The Unbearable typical Scottish g

Before we begin;

In my hand I hold a wood
I swing it smooth the way I should
It seems so easy first of all
To strike that tiny dimpled ball

Why then should it rarely be
It lands somewhere that I can see
With acres of green on which to land
Why does it mostly prefer the sand?

Why does it, on a whim
Strike a tree or try to swim
Its favourite game is hide and seek
But need it be, every week

It is my only heartfelt aim
To master this infernal game
This evil game that haunts my soul
With its narrow fairways and tiny hole

I lose my calm and sense of reason
At the start of every golfing season
The route I take I know so well
The slippery slope to golfing hell

I hook I slice I shank I duff
Help me please I've had enough
Why does this game cause so much sorrow
Perhaps it won't when I play tomorrow.

Warning;

You may at some points in this book imagine or presume that one of the characters is based on you, it isn't. All characters and situations are entirely fictional and pure made up. If you do think somebody in the book sounds like you or acts like you then you're wrong, get over yourself, as if anybody would write about you anyway.

There is an index of fictional members and their nicknames at the back of the book if anybody is interested, in fact it will still be there even if you're not interested. Please remember these people do not exist, they are not real, they are figments of my imagination only.

Dedicated to golf society golfers everywhere, to all the intrepid members who see hurricanes as blustery showers that will blow over in a minute and who see a layer of ice on the course as a benefit to distance achievable, rather than a hindrance. To any golfer that has had to prise their fingers from a club due to frostbite or anyone who has ever played Carnoustie golf course on a day with horizontal hailstones and with a wind chill factor of minus twelve. (Been there done that.)

Dedication; This book is dedicated to William; you know who you are, thanks for the inspiration.

Introduction;

My name is Danny McCallister; I am a Sunday golfer.

Rather like an alcoholic I think it's important that you know that I suffer from an affliction. I am an addict, a golf addict and that might put some of the nonsense that follows in some context. I am assuming the majority of people who have opened the cover and looked this far are Golfers or at least interested in golf. Welcome to those of you who are members of golf societies and to the more sensible amongst you who aren't.

The following chapters will chronicle my journey from friendly human being to rabid golf society member. Please read this and take heed, if anyone ever approaches you and says "We have a wee golf society, a few old boys that get together on a Sunday morning and bash a ball about a wee bit, do you fancy joining us?" Smile politely and back away slowly, do not in any way indicate that you are interested, and then run! As fast as you can and don't look back.

Golf in itself is a wickedly deceptive game, it allows you to feel that you may be getting a semblance of partial control before it cruelly reminds you that the god's of golf are in charge and don't you forget it. It can be almost mastered look at the sheer number of golf pro's. That level of golf of course is not the level we inhabit, the Sunday golfers, oh no, we inhabit an altogether different world, where we know we should practice more, but why waste your time, when you can buy magic birdie beans from the gypsy lady, or as they are more commonly known, golf gadgets.

Why practice bunker shot's when it is clear to even the most basic idiot that there are at least ten problems with bunkers, 1.Too little sand, in the bunker, 2.Too much sand in the bunker, 3. The sand is too wet. 4. The sand is too dry. 5. The sand is the wrong type. 6. The sand was stolen from a building site and dumped in the bunker. 7. The sand is too soft. 8. The sand is too hard. 9. The stones are bigger than golf balls. 10. Bunkers are not necessary to enjoy a game of golf.

Why put any time into practicing putting, most pro-shops have second hand putters from about twenty five quid and they have loads of them, everybody's ideal putter is out there it just takes time to find it.

And a couple of things to remember three swings of a golf club and a stretch of the back whilst screaming aagh does not constitute a warm up, and finally please don't forget the less skilled a player is, the more likely he is to share his ideas about your golf swing.

How it all began;

"Da, there's a member of the golf club here who stays around the corner from me, David Simpson he's gave us a shout and asked if we fancy coming along on Sunday mornings for a game, him and a bunch of other guys have a wee golf society they call themselves "The Unbearables" they play every week and they are looking for new people to join them, do you fancy it?" my son Peter innocently asked me.

We had recently joined Happy Valley Golf Club just outside Kirkintilloch where we lived, and were standing on the practice putting green waiting in a longish queue for our tee time. A very dark cloud passed over the sun and brought with it a cold wind, even though it had been a glorious Saturday afternoon in July just moments before. It would have been easy to feel that chill wind and recognise it as an omen, we didn't, I didn't, I should have.

"It's not a bad idea I suppose Peter, that's why it's so hard to get a tee time here on a Sunday, they have quite a few of those wee societies and they seem to get priority over everybody else, so why not, what harm can it do"

I was forty eight Peter was twenty eight, how could we be so damned naive.

Or maybe we weren't naive, maybe we believed in the milk of human kindness, maybe we believed that most people are decent ordinary hard working human beings like ourselves, but then we hadn't yet met or come to know The Unbearables.

But we would, in a very short time we would know them well, too well.

Chapter one; Empty your pockets, you belong to us now.

A friend of ours who had joined the club at the same time as us, Charlie Gilhooley, also came along with us that fateful Sunday morning, basically for the same reasons as us, a chance for a regular tee time and I suppose an opportunity to get to know some other members of the club. Charlie quickly became known as "Cavalier" not because of the cavalier way he approached golf insisting that he didn't actually care about winning or losing he only cared about making the perfect shot, no he was called the Cavalier because he laughed uproariously at anything, basically comedians should pay him to turn up at their shows, there's nothing he doesn't laugh at, except bunkers I suppose, he doesn't find them all that funny.

All three of us turned up at the same time and thus entered the "smokers room" together precisely seven forty five am. There is a rule you see, which is sacrosanct, if you aren't there at eight o'clock on the dot, your name doesn't go into the draw and you don't play, unless of course you are in one of the numerous cliques and somebody puts your card in for you. There was no shortage of local rules and customs all of which would eventually be explained to us, usually when we required an explanation as to why we had lost another pound.

"How are you guys doing, David said there was a couple of new boys interested in joining. It's a tenner each, and a pound for the sweep" said Pat McGee the organiser/ treasurer/ all round dogsbody and secretary of the Unbearables.

As we each opened our wallets and handed him a tenner (actually I handed him a twenty, when Peter asked me to pay his as he had no money with him, a recurring problem, rather like royalty Peter doesn't carry cash very often, also like royalty he believes it his position to enjoy life and my position to pay for it) Pat McGee accepted the notes with a smile and made them disappear into his pocket with all the dexterity of Derren Brown on speed.

"And don't forget your six quid for the two's" a rather portly red faced figure in the corner piped up and held out and jangled a plastic tub full of one pound coins in our direction.

I looked at the portly guy trying to decide if he was at the wind up, I know his type, in fact I am his type, but apparently he wasn't at the wind up, this time. They had a weekly competition in which everybody paid a pound each week and anybody who scored a two at the eighteenth hole got a share of the accumulated money, which currently hadn't been won in the previous five weeks and therefore it was six pounds each if we wished to enter and by the look on the faces of the other unbearables it wasn't voluntary it was mandatory. There is only one player who doesn't enter the two's and he is probably the player who most frequently gets two's, apart of course from Lesley Clifford, (you will meet him later) who actually declares the two's money as taxable income he wins so much of it.

I reluctantly took another tenner out along with a couple of pound coins and threw them into the proffered plastic sandwich tub, they were accepted by Andy Ingles with a smile that when he shared with his immediate neighbours alerted me to the fact that I may have been gently mugged. As I Looked round the smokers room, which actually wasn't a smokers room it had just always been called that, it was what most clubs called the wet bar an area you could come into straight from the course, the members lounge requires proper attire and footwear. I could see three or four distinct groups, their hierarchy would become more obvious as the weeks progressed. As at any golf club breeches of that hierarchy were taken very seriously, woe betide the player who tried to get on the first tee before the old boys club on a Saturday morning.

The smoker's room consist of a bar, two large screen televisions and about five or six tables arranged along the wall opposite the bar and around a bay window at the end of the room. The most noticeable and loudest group were seated at the tables at the bay window, this mob apparently were called the Peasies, a sub division of the Unbearables after four years I still haven't really found out why they are called the Peasies I am presuming it has to do with them being from Petersburn rather than anything to do with their toiletry habits, or the fact that they are generally easy peasy to beat in team competitions like Texas scrambles.

There was a group of golfers gathered at the tables opposite the bar, this consisted of five men who had a combined age of almost four hundred, do the maths, four hundred divided by five means that their average age was approaching eighty. FFS eighty, I mean really, why weren't they in a rest home somewhere, talk about one foot in the grave or what. In saying that they all looked as fit as butchers dogs and I would learn to my cost that they all still had a good game in them.

Pat McGee stood up and made an announcement "I know it's a bit early but I am looking at Ayrshire for next year's winter league outing so if anybody has any course preferences or wants to start paying up for the outing just let me know" He carried on talking for a few minutes about what courses and what hotel and various other arrangements but It seemed to me that it was only Peter, Charlie and I that paid him any attention the rest responded as if he was just background noise.

"Right it's nearly eight O'clock let's get this draw done, so can everybody shut the fuck up for a minute and listen for your name coming out, we don't want a repeat of last week, when we ended up with a five ball going out last, because one of the old bastards wisnae listening" this announcement came from Jasper Lemon also known as bozo because as his fellow peasie Andy Ingles (the fat guy guarding the two's money)explained, every circus needs a clown, I am not sure if this was an ironic nickname because even though he thinks he's funny he isn't or the nickname stuck because if anybody was to pull an unfunny practical joke like unplugging your trolley battery or bursting a balloon behind your head it would be Jasper, like the time he poked my golf brolly into one of the club spaces in my golf bag and then opened the brolly meaning I couldn't get it back out, or indeed get any of my clubs back in. I haven't had my revenge for that yet but I will.

"Right there are sixteen here today so that means a three ball and three four balls" Jasper began shuffling the score cards in preparation for the draw.

"Surely if there's sixteen that means four times four balls, where the fuck are you getting a three ball from, you fucking fanny" asked Andy Ingles also known as the fat controller, because he controlled the two's competition and mainly because he was fat.

Jasper laid the cards out in front of him and put them into four piles of four and said "Oh aye so it is, there you go then that's four four balls picked I'll just read out the names"

"No you fuckin won't" Interjected a sturdy guy walking into the smoking room swigging from a can of lager, "You're no putting me in the last game again, every fucking week I go out for a fag or a quick shite and when I come back in, I'm in the last fuckin game"

9

This was Bart Cooper also known as the fat ugly bin man, due to an incident at a previous golf outing when he been refused service at a hotel bar, which in his loud and outspoken opinion was because he was a fat ugly bin man, whilst in the barman's opinion he wasn't being served because he was absolutely pished it was four o'clock in the morning and that he was bollock naked.

"For fuck sake, ok I'll do the draw again, David are you going out with the three new guys" Jasper asked pausing for an answer as David Simpson, Peter's neighbour who had invited us along broke off his conversation with the big guy sitting beside him and looked at the three of us and asked "What handicaps are yous three"

I responded for all of us "21, 16 and 15" Pointing at Peter Charlie and then myself.

David turned back to Jasper and said "Naw" and then carried on with his conversation. Charmer.

Jasper looked at the two people either side of him and when they both shrugged their shoulders he did the same and commenced the draw. It turned out that Peter and I were out in the first four ball with two of the older boys and Charlie was out in the last game, let the fun and games begin.

"Are we having a doubles match" Barry Monk asked, he was one of the old boys, we had been drawn to play with.

"Aye if you want" Peter responded "why not, how much is it for, me and my Da will play yous two"

"It's only a pound son" Barry replied with a twinkle in his eye, and scurried away to the first tee with a spring in his step, a spring which to be fair was there constantly rain or shine. If Barry had a tail it would constantly be wagging. I can only hope to have half of that energy and enthusiasm when I grow up.

Let me take just a minute to explain this "only a pound", it is in reality, a pound coin which everybody pays into the sweep when you lose your match on a Sunday, when you win your match your opponent "the loser" pays your pound along with his own pound. It sounds insignificant doesn't it, a pound, a simple little pound coin which wouldn't even buy you a cup of coffee these days. Why then did grown men curse, swear, throw tantrums, break clubs and inflict violence on bags, trolleys and tee boxes because they were in danger of losing a pound? Because it wasn't the value it was the symbolism. Walking into the smokers room and putting your two quid on the table after your match symbolises that you are a loser. Walking in and not putting your two quid on the table doesn't really make you a winner because that two quid goes into the sweep to be collected by the top scorers of the day, it just means that you aren't a loser (that day).

"You were a bit quick accepting a match there Peter, I suppose you're gonny pay the pounds when we lose are you" I said sarcastically as I already knew to my cost this was one of Peter's cashless days. Strangely Peter is generous to a fault with everyone else, it's just me he scams, he takes after his mother I suppose.

"Look at them" Peter said, smiling. That old guy Barry is bouncing about like a puppy with two tails and that other old yin, Jack Sharp is it, he hasn't even made it to the first tee before he's had to go behind a bush for a pish, we'll beat them easy" The naivety of youth.

As we got prepared to play Jack Sharp took a Marks and Spencer's carrier bag out of the side pocket of his golf bag and began rummaging through it.

"Great stuff" I thought, they are going to have a bloody picnic before we even start.

As I meandered onto the tee I noticed in fact that the carrier bag was full of tee pegs, roughly, I would imagine about a thousand of them. Jack laid a few out on top of the green litter bin by the tee, clearly making his selection for the day. There were tees of every imaginable length and colour, there were some in the shape of naked ladies and at least a couple which resembled a male Adonis. There were some with string attached and a set of, what I later discovered, were winter tees, 3 little upside down egg cups tied together, the theory, I assume, being that when the ground was too hard to press in a tee these could be used.

He carefully selected his bundle of tees and put them in his pocket, I asked "Have you got enough there Jack"

He looked at me and smiled "Tees are like women son, they come in all shapes and sizes and you canny have too many"

"Aye right, Peter, this will be easy" I thought, I was willing to give odds that these two auld yins knew their way round the course and we might just get our arses skelped if we weren't careful.

A coin was tossed, we got to tee off first. I teed up and swung my driver at the ball in my usual ham fisted way which I considered was styled on Colin Montgomery low and hard, it actually looked more like Field Marshall Montgomery trying to swat a fly.

My ball decided that as there was water and out of bounds on my left that it would do the sensible thing and head straight right, as I breathed in and got ready to bellow a warning a short sharp shout was let out behind me "FORE LEFT"

I jumped a little and turned round to see Barry Monk smiling at me.

"My ball went right, it was heading for the end of the trees over there" I said pointing to the right hand side of the fairway.

"Oh no son, you went left, I seen it I was keeping my eye on it, I'm a champion at watching the ball I'm telling you, your ball went left, right behind that tree over there on the left, I can practically see it just now, son" Barry said adamantly.

He had me doubting my own vision, I turned and looked at Peter who shrugged his shoulders he was too busy adjusting his new Nike golf glove which matched his new Nike golf trousers that he had bought to match his new Nike polo shirt. I turned further to ask Jack Sharp if he had seen my ball, but he obviously hadn't because he had his back to us whilst he did his second pish of the round into the bush beside the first tee.

"Is it me to go, sorry I just need a wee pee there" Gentleman Jack Sharp explained, as he adjusted his bits and straightened his trouser leg.

Without waiting for an answer he stepped on to the tee, put his ball on a peg, bent over to press it into the grass wobbled for a bit and then eventually made his way into the upright position where he had started, stood up straight and then almost without pausing whacked it straight down the middle.

"No it's actually me to go but it doesn't matter" Peter said approaching the tee.

Peter made sure his Nike glove was pulled on tight and that his Nike trousers were sitting just right on his Nike shoes and then addressed his ball and paused, and then paused a little longer and then finally paused a wee bit more before unleashing a ferocious swipe at the ball sending it a hundred yards to his left into some trees. Through his swing every part of his body moved except his bowels.

"Great shot son, that was worth waiting for, definitely great shot son, I seen where it went, super shot." Barry said, getting ready to play his tee shot.

He teed up his ball took half a swing back to line himself up properly and then battered his ball down the middle, "Did you see that son that was a great shot wasn't it, did you see it son, I got through that okay, did you see the ball flight, it was great wasn't it son" He said as he scurried off the tee and started pushing his trolley towards the fairway.

My ball was very much in the trees on the right and not over on the left Barry didn't offer any explanation for his insistence that the ball was on the left, he was too busy looking in a bush for Peter's ball which was found about forty yards further on from where Barry was looking.

"Fivfafor" Barry chirped when his six foot putt ran round the rim and fell in the hole at the first. "One up"

"What?" I asked looking at Pater slightly bewildered, as I had just tapped in for a five.

"I'm stroking here son, five for four, we go one up" Barry said with a mischievous twinkle and scurried away to the second tee.

The whole match basically followed the same pattern, I would think we had done ok on a hole and Barry would chirrup "Fivfafor" or "forfarthree" and swagger away. We lost three and two, unsurprisingly. Also unsurprisingly Barry Monk's nickname is Hawkeye.

Sitting relaxing in the clubhouse after our first match in the Unbearables summer league we reflected on how our induction had gone.

"Well that wasn't too bad was it" Peter asked tucking into his cheese toasty.

"No, not if you don't mind being stung by a couple of old pensioners for a pound" I said lamenting the emptiness of my pockets, for some strange reason Peter had forgot his bar card as well as his money today so the drinks were on me as well.

"I don't think they stung us, they just beat us" Peter said magnanimously.

"If we weren't stung, how come wee Barry seemed to be getting a stroke at every hole then?" I asked bewildered. "All we heard out of him was fivfafor, sixfafiv, It got on my nerves to be honest" "And another thing Jack sharp might need to piss at every hole but it didnae put him off did it, he had a par on the first four holes on the back nine that's why they did us, I think he's an old rogue, on every single hole one of them had a par at least, and he disnae miss a trick does he, he's a sharp old codger I'll tell you that for nothing."

"It wisnae every hole, you're exaggerating, you need to work on that angry wee man chip on your shoulder" Peter offered as his advice.

"I'll fuckin angry wee man you, what are you talking about" I berated him aggressively.

"See" he said. He sounds like his mother as well sometimes.

This amused Charlie Gilhooley who had by this time joined us, but as I said earlier practically everything amused Charlie.

"Who were you out with and how did you get on" Peter asked Charlie, whilst I tried to bring this imaginary anger under control.

Charlie laughed (Naturally) and said "Wee oily, big oily and the fat ugly bin man"

It was our turn to both laugh and before Peter finished saying "who the fuc.." Charlie explained, "Those two guys over there, the big guy and the wee guy sitting at the window, one of them's called Barney Piper, he's a plumber of course with a name like that what else would he be, and the other one's called Billy Paterson, so both of their initials are BP, so do you get it BP, oil, big oily and wee oily" he then laughed loud enough to rattle the windows and put the guy on the eighteenth green off his putt. The guy stared at the window for about a minute presumably wanting somebody to blame for his shit putt. Andy Ingles the fat controller summed him up quite well "Fanny" he said dismissively.

All in all it couldn't be said to be a bad start, all three of us had enjoyed the golf, but on the down side my wallet was considerably lighter than when I came in but hey ho, the banter had been good.

Just as we pushed our chairs back to leave, Peter's arm was grabbed by Jamie MacArthur who asked "Are you leaving them son" pointing at some crisps Peter had left on his plate.

"Aw for fuck sake conductor will you stop fuckin begging for food" Andy Ingles shouted at him. The conductor gently giggled and lifted the plate over to where he was sitting and tucked in. The Conductor was Jamie McArthur, so called because of the silky tempo of his swing rather than any resemblance he might have had to Stan's mate Jack Harper in "On the Buses".

By the end of that summer which was an extremely warm one, we had pretty much played at least a couple of rounds with all of the participants in the unbearables, with growing success, all of us had only recently received official handicaps when joining Happy Valley Golf Club, which to be honest were probably slightly, very slightly, generous. This meant that we were slowly building up quite a nice pot of winnings which we called "the tin", we had decided that the three of us would pool whatever winnings we had each week and use any proceeds to help pay for the winter league golf outing which was increasingly becoming the main topic of conversation.

On one of the early Sundays of the winter league Peter and I were drawn out in a four ball with porky part one and porky part two, that would be Stuart Taggart and Baxter Carter. Who were both policeman hence the nicknames. They were completely different types of policemen, one thought the best way to question criminals was to throw them down the stairs head first and then they would tell you what you needed to know, the other thought it best to persuade the criminals to throw themselves down the stairs and then let them tell you what you needed to know.

It was a wet and very blustery day at Happy Valley Golf Club, most people wouldn't leave the house to go to the shops on mornings like this, but twelve of our hardy mob had turned up. As they piled on multiple layers of waterproof clothing and got ready to play golf it resembled an expeditionary force preparing for a final assault on the south face of the Matterhorn, had a Sherpa turned up with ropes I think he would have fitted right in.

"What game am I in son" Barry Monk asked looking up from his coffee. "I'm not sure if I'm even bothering to go out yet"

"You're in the last game Barry, with me and them two" Charlie Gilhooley said with a huge laugh (as per usual), pointing at the conductor and Bozo. The conductor was currently trying on a new balaclava which could also be transformed into a hat, it was currently half and half, the result being that he bumped into a table when the thing covered his eyes, spilling my coffee and Andy Ingle's can of Tennant's super lager.

"Aw for fuck's sake Conductor, is your carer no here yet, Jesus Christ that's a fucking waste look at my can its half empty"

"Aye and you spilt half my coffee as well auld yin" I said, happy to join in bating the Conductor.

And Ingles gave me a look of despair "I think you and me have to have a wee talk son" he said ominously "If you think that spilling coffee is in the same league as spilling my breakfast can, then me and thee are going to fall out, I noticed you grabbed your coffee cup when stupid arse bumped into the table, I didnae notice you trying to save my can, that says thing's about your character that are a bit suspect if you ask me, anybody that puts coffee in front of lager is one to be watched I think."

"Right who's on the tee, come on the tee's empty, let's get moving or we will miss our slot" Jasper Lemon bawled.

"What is the matter with you, ya fanny, we're the only people stupid enough to be here, who do you think is gonny jump in before us, Hilary Fucking Tensing." Farqhuarson Dixon said laughing.

"Right that's it then, somebody else can do the draw in the mornings, nobody listens, then everybody moans and now when I try to get you'se all moving I get called a fanny, if I wisnae here, you'se widnae even have a draw most mornings" Jasper Lemon bemoaned.

"It would be a price worth paying" I said Sotto Voce, but just loud enough to be heard, it brought a huge grin to the face of Jasper Lemon and calmed his ire.

As I said I was out with Peter and the two porky's, we were first out. We should have known better than to continue, to get on to the first tee at Happy Valley you cross a short path and go through a four bar gate, it took two of us to push open the gate the wind was so fierce. Once through the gate it was a walk of fifty or so yards to the first tee, by the time we reached it I looked and felt as if I had jumped in a swimming pool with all of my clothes on, it was ludicrous that we had ventured even this far. I was on the tee, I looked at Peter basically trying to confirm my insanity or at least to confirm that I wasn't the only madman, he shrugged his shoulders, I swished the club backwards and forwards twice, this constituted my entire warm up routine. I shook my head in for a penny and all that. As the wind was so fierce I visualised a low flat swing in an attempt to keep the ball low and cut through the wind like a knife through butter. Big swing, missed the ball completely, half spun round and just avoided falling on my arse.

"You missed it" said Porky one, (Stuart Taggart).

I glared at him "I can see why you made detective " I said "There's not much gets past you does it, I know I fucking missed it, there was a wee let up in the fuckin hurricane that's why I fuckin missed it Columbo"

"Was it no just a really real looking practice swing Da" Peter asked, straight faced. Porky Two sniggered.

It was difficult to know where to direct my next glare, I opted for porky two and said "I don't suppose you noticed me missing it did you, after all you're no a detective you're just a plod so you were too busy thinking about what time Greggs opens, eh."

He absorbed this with a vacant smile, obviously I had put the thought of a steak bake in his mind and he was happy.

We all eventually managed to get off the tee and were bent double into the wind pushing our golf trolley's the hundred or so yards to where our drives had landed.

Peter shouted into the wind "Da, the rest of them have just walked off the first tee and went back to the clubhouse"

The four of us all turned round and watched them trudge back up the path, with the howling wind at their back they were struggling to hold on to their trolleys.

"I suppose we better go off as well then" Stuart Taggart shouted at me, even though he was less than ten feet away.

"Are you conceding the match then" I asked anticipating an easy pound.

He laughed and turned away towards his ball, I caught up with him as he bent to pick his ball up.

"Are you conceding the match" I asked again holding his arm to prevent him lifting his ball.

"Are you fuckin kidding" he asked, "it's blowing a fucking gale, the rain is of fucking monsoon standard the here will probably be a tsunami coming up the Kelvin in a minute let's get to fuck before we drown"

"Gimme the pounds then" I said, holding my hand out.

"We are all chucking it, so nobody has to pay" he said.

"I don't think so" I replied "I'm happy to play on, I feel as if I might play well the day, so what's your choice, are you going in and paying up, or are you playing on"

"What kind of drugs are you on wee man" Stuart asked "You had a fresh air and then hit the ball seventy yards with your driver, what the fuck makes you think you're gonny play well the day"

"Optimism" I said and held out my hand, into which he dropped two quid, I think I was getting the hang of this summer/winter league thing.

Chapter two; The rest of the Asylum

There were almost thirty players in the unbearables when we first joined. Thanks to the system of basically drawing four names out of a hat every Sunday morning, it wasn't long before we had played a few rounds with each of them, let me tell you about some of the more memorable rounds.

Before I do just a mention for the club pro's at Happy Valley, Stan and Oliver. It is always a good idea to keep these guys sweet, when you forget to book into a medal and are looking at a five o'clock tee on a Saturday night, it's then, that you are glad you bought a few things from the shop and had a lesson or two to ingratiate yourself with the guys that control the start times.

Stan had the nose of a blood hound, the kitchens at Happy Valley have this weird tradition of having no wish to make money before ten a.m. so despite the fact that there are approximately forty to fifty members who go out every Saturday and Sunday before 9.am they do so without a bacon roll or a decent coffee. This is where Stan's ability comes in, every so often this lack of a bacon roll makes me visit the drive through MacDonald's on the way to the course, where I generally buy three coffees and three breakfast rolls, for Charlie, Peter and me.

As soon as I arrive at the course and open the car door, Stan is in the vicinity.

"What's that?" he asks nodding at the MacDonald's brown paper bag in my hand.

"It's a monkey on roller skates" I reply.

"Did you get me a roll and bacon" he asks, licking his lips.

"Naw" I answer him brutally.

"You knew I was here, I'm always here and you always forget" he says petulantly.

"I know the green keepers got two dogs but I don't bring them biscuits, do I" I answer.

As Stan walks away, disconsolately, I call after him "What time did Peter book us on"

"He didnae" Stan answered, just as Peter arrived and stepped out of his car.

"Aye I did" Peter shouted across "It was for 8.07"

"Prove it" Stan called back and turned to me and grinned.

Oliver on the other hand was a much more agreeable chap. It was a regular thing to have a pleasant conversation with him as you browsed the goodies in the pro-shop.

"Oliver, is this new Taylor Made Driver any good" I asked.

"Yeah, yeah" he answered

"What about the ping driver, have you heard good things about that yet" I asked.

"Yeah, yeah" he answered.

"I might change my driver this year, I've got an old R7, and I hit it straight but no distance to speak of really" I said

"Yeah, yeah" he replied.

"I might just take a lesson first but, in case it's me and my swing rather than the driver"

"Yeah, yeah" he said.

"OK then, I'll have a think about it, if I do want to change my driver, I'll give you a shout and book a lesson, cheers for the advice"

"Yeah, yeah" he said.

Told you he's a very agreeable guy, who is always a delight to talk to. Joking Aside, he fitted me for my clubs and is very very good with the technical stuff most of which went over my head, but it was very good, yeah yeah.

Stan also once told me a story about a guy who used to be a member, Alan Marshall his name was, unfortunately Alan Died before I joined Happy Valley, there's a lovely bench at the fourteenth tee dedicated to him and he seems to have been held in extremely high regard, by many of the members.

According to Stan, he was giving someone a chipping lesson down at the practice area when Alan came along and stood watching. The person getting the lesson was abysmal. He either hit the ball six inches in front of him or shanked it wildly. Stan persevered, trying to show the guy the fundamentals, like choke down on the grip, stay open and narrow, ball back in the stance weight on your forward side, he was trying everything, his pupil just wasn't getting it.

Alan approached him and said "Have you thought of shortening the shafts by about three inches"

Stan looked at him in puzzlement "Why would that make any difference"

The pupil, who having had six lessons already from Stan and was getting absolutely nowhere, and was therefore willing to listen to practically anything that gave him a semblance of hope in getting rid of his shank problem asked Alan "Do you think that would make a difference to my weight distribution big man, or would it help me to shorten my swing plane or something"

Alan shook his head and smiled as he answered, "No pal it wouldn't but it would mean that you would be able to shut the wheelie bin lid, when you throw your clubs in it."

One of Stan's most endearing tricks is to stand beside you having a pleasant chat while you hit a few practice putts on the practice green whilst waiting for your tee time, he will sometimes slip in a comment like "Stop wiggling your arse when you putt" or "maintain the V through the putt" which is all very helpful, until you check your account in the pro shop and find out he has charged you for a lesson. I love it when he does that, it gives me a warm glow inside to know that I have paid for his next MacDonalds.

....

Middle of August, nice weather, dry and reasonably warm but with a slight breeze, I have been drawn out with Pat McGee (our Great leader), so called because in his head that's what he sees himself as, and to be fair he did run the society basically single handed, to be unfair he would struggle to lead an old woman across a busy road.

Ingram Houston, Ingram had a couple of nicknames firstly he was known as Squidward a character from the cartoon Sponge Bob Square Pants this was because someone had once described Ingram's swing as resembling an octopus falling out of a tree, he was also occasionally called the spanner, due to the degree of difficulty involved in trying to get a fifty pence piece out of his hand.

He is the one that never enters the two's despite the fact that he has just as many if not more two's than anybody else. The fourth player that morning was the smiler, Ivan Bentley, so called because whatever circumstances he was presented with his reaction was always a smile.

I was paired with Pat McGee, which normally gives you a better than even chance of winning thanks to Pat's phobia, apparently he had a childish fear of the number six and on his therapists advice always wrote down five instead of the scary number whenever he could, on his card of course the fear disappeared when marking anybody else's score, a strange phenomena these phobia's aren't they.

Ingram Houston teed up at the first, took a couple of practice swings that according to the laws of physics should actually have screwed him slightly into the ground but didn't, he then launched his club at the ball and hooked it straight out of bounds and into the river Kelvin. Silence on the tee.

He stomped to his bag and carefully selected another ball, teed up went through the same routine and again hooked it straight out of bounds on such a similar line that there was a fair chance both balls could be lying touching on the river bed.

He turned to us with complete frustration on his face and said "They have made this a really difficult hole, cutting the fairways in like that" and stomped away to get a third ball. To our eternal credit none of us laughed out loud although Ivan's Smile went from forty watts to a hundred watts.

After five holes we were all square and walking up the sixth fairway to play our second shots, well I say the sixth fairway but my drive was a lot closer to the seventh fairway which ran parallel with the sixth, as I approached my drive I noticed Jack Sharp in the bunker on the seventh fairway, and in the bunker beside him was his electric trolley complete with bag and clubs.

"What happened Jack, are you ok" I asked genuinely concerned as I walked over towards him, I thought he must have tripped and fallen.

"Aye son, I'm fine" he answered, as he looked from side to side in the bunker shaking his head. He turned to look at me and said "I duffed my second shot into the bunker and when I got in to play it, I couldn't have switched my trolley off, and the next thing I knew was that my trolley was in beside me and then it tipped over spilling all the balls out of the pouch at the bottom.

As I reached the bunker I noticed that there were about a couple of dozen balls randomly scattered in it. "Here let me help you pick them up, I thought maybe you had fallen or something, as long as you're ok, that's good"

He turned away from me and said "Oh you can't pick them up yet, I'm still trying to decide which ball is the one I was playing" I left him there, bending over and straining to see the markings on the balls. I at least managed to walk thirty yards away before bursting into laughter, which I mostly held in.

Pat McGee was standing over his ball which was slightly behind a tree obscuring his route to the green, "I will take a drop here Danny" he said stooping to lift the ball.

"Why, what's up is the tree in your way" I said laughing. Thinking wrongly that I was being sarcastic.

"No it's all these animal droppings" he said indicating some rabbit shit at his feet.

I looked him squarely in the eye and asked "What the fuck are you talking about?"

"Those animal dropping" he said "they are interfering with my stance"

"Well I suppose you might have a point Pat" I said feigning being agreeable "If your normal stance is to play in your bare feet with your legs six feet apart" Which come to think of it isn't the worst stance I have seen on this course. It's not even the worst stance I have tried.

"Or is it the smell of the animal droppings that are putting you off" I asked "Because if it is then maybe what you can actually smell is the bullshit coming out of your mouth" I walked away with a grin on my face because I like my own jokes.

"You're supposed to be on my side" he whined.

"Take a drop then" I advised "We can always check in the pro shop when we finish, both Stan and Oliver are in today" as you know Stan and Oliver are the club pro's, who we normally ask for rulings.

Pat played his shot as it lay, I shook my head and grinned again. Fanny.

As it happens it made little difference to the outcome, Pat and I won four and three, thanks mainly to Ivan and Ingram's poor putting on the day, rather than us doing anything special. But it did give me a heads up on what to look out for.

The following week Charlie Gilhooley and I were paired with, Lesley Clifford and Walter Hagen, two of the better golfers in the society, both play off low handicaps and are very consistent and talented golfers. Lesley would later go on to become club champion, thanks mainly to a motivational speech I gave him when he was half way through his match in the final, I told him as I passed him on the third fairway "Reaching the final is a great achievement big guy so don't worry if you get humped, you won't really be a loser, well none of us will think so anyway, well not many of us" I think that spurred him on to his triumph. Actually that same summer, the second tier club championship for players with a handicap of more than nine, was also won by a member of our little society, Gary Royal, who was immediately given the nickname Bra strap, on the basis that he was the holder of the diddy cup.

Both Lesley and Walter proved that my theory about low handicap golfers was wrong, I had a theory that the lower a players handicap then the higher the chance that he is a fanny or arrogant dickhead, I think my theory might be based on jealousy and envy. Neither of them fitted the natural stereotype of good golfers, tall athletic handsome, that would be a no on all three counts. Lesley is above average height I suppose, in fact he has grown right through his hair, Walter is of a similar build to myself short and chunky, the difference being he has a golf swing and a short game to admire, I have a swing that looks like a caveman killing his lunch and a short game which can go from ice cold to lukewarm in the swish of a club.

The real beauty of golf is that thanks to the handicap system, mediocre golfers like me and Charlie (who is improving rapidly, and showing some small signs of becoming a fanny in the process) can actually compete against superior low handicap golfers like Lesley and Walter, the handicap system is designed to give us a chance to pit our skills and wits against anybody, on a level playing field. It was a little surprising then that we found ourselves six down through six holes, so much for all that pish about the handicaps making it even, they were annihilating us, we then steadied (when I say we, I mean Charlie) we halved the next hole and won two out of the next three, leaving us four down with eight to play, not a great position to be in but better than we deserved.

On the eleventh tee Lesley Clifford mentioned to Walter Hagen that he had bumped into Walter's ex wife in the supermarket, he then asked Walter if they were getting on any better these days. Walter who was approaching his tee shot went a deep red in the face, which went away when he started breathing normally again and he said "Naw" teed up squared up and blasted his ball seventy yards right of the fairway into an area of trees never to be seen again. He again went red in the face and I could see his knuckles going white as he walked towards his bag to get another ball.

Lesley in the meantime played his tee shot, a rather slicey weak effort for him, caused, I think, by his attention being on Walter Hagen who was standing by his bag selecting a provisional ball, but as he rummaged through his ball bag, he seemed to be getting angrier and angrier, by the time he had teed up his second ball I would swear in a court of law there was steam coming out of every orifice. I don't have a clue where that second ball went, he hit it so hard that there is every possibility he sent it into orbit, or it disintegrated into matter and anti matter, he picked up his pink tee and said "N.R" and walked off towards the next hole.

We won the hole, we were now only three down, but Walters reaction to Lesley mentioning his ex had cast a bit of a shadow over the game, by the time we were on the next tee, Walter appeared to have settled down and hit his usual splendid drive down the middle, that basically allowed the rest of us to play vaguely normal shots. Lesley and Charlie boomed two drives on to the edge of the twelfth green and I sliced my drive onto the thirteenth fairway, as I said normal tee shots for all of us.

Being a friendly sort of person, interested in the well being of my pals, I asked Walter an innocent question as he stood over his second shot.

"What was that all about on the last tee, you went mental, was that something to do with your ex?" I smiled.

Walter played his second shot with a sand wedge he was roughly about sixty yards from the middle of the green, in my conservative estimate I would say he hit the ball just over two hundred and ten yards, up and over the twelfth green , the eleventh green and the ninth fairway. It was just about the length of one of my best drives. He glared at me as if I had done something wrong rather than just asking a completely innocent question.

When he regained his composure slightly, he did in fact relay the fact that his divorce had been slightly problematic, when he said slightly problematic I think he meant the way that Al Qaeda and the American military had a problematic relationship. I later found out that a year or so previously Walter had come up to Happy Valley on a Sunday morning as usual, the weather on the drive up had been wet and windy but not that bad for Scotland in the winter. But when he got to the course the rain was coming down in torrents and the wind was of hurricane proportions, despite several protests from the winter league boys, Walter amongst them, the course was closed for the day by the green keeping staff.

Walter then at a loss what to do decided he would go home sneak back into bed and hope for a Sunday morning special. So he did, he drove home was very careful slipping his key quietly into the lock, pushed the door open slowly, making sure it didn't creak. He slipped off his shoes and climbed the stairs, again making sure he avoided the fourth step which squeaked like a cat having its tail stood on. So far so good, he pushed the bedroom door open and could hear his wife gently snoring, so he slipped in behind her and put his arms around her cupping one of her breasts and whispered in her ear "It's raining cats and dogs out there."

And his wife replied "I know I can hear it, and that stupid bastard Walter's away playing golf in it"

Obviously that was the final straw for them and they split up quite soon after, not of course in an amicable way, it's safe to say they weren't going to be friends anytime this millennium. There was a separate rumour that the guy she had been expecting that morning may well have been a fellow member of the Unbearables, but more about that later.

Whatever, I had now had his button and would be happy to press it at will, I must find out her name maybe even try and find a photo, just in case I ever draw Walter in the singles. Walter's son Randy Hagen is a completely different character much more laid back and less temperamental in fact in many ways he reminds me more of Bart Cooper than his dad, except in looks, Shagger is much better looking than Bart Cooper and better dressed with his fancy belts and his fancy watch.

Lesley and Charlie managed to both make par on the twelfth, having recovered from their shock at seeing Walter's wedge shot travelling at half the speed of light. We then halved the thirteenth leaving Charlie and I now three down with five to play, it was getting close to where we would need to concede defeat so I asked Charlie quietly "Walter's finished what can we do to get Lesley to crumble. Charlie looked at me with shock.

"What do you mean" he asked "try and put him off, that's terrible"

"It is when you put it that way" I answered "I never said we should try and put him off, just help him put himself off, you know what I mean, like whenever you are playing against me and you land in a bunker, I always come over and look at your ball and shake my head and say, that's a bloody awful lie, and that makes you tighten your grip and thrash at the ball a bit, which usually means most of the time you play a shite bunker shot"

He looked at me warily not sure whether I was winding him up or not, he reacted the way I would normally expect him to react and barked out a very loud laugh, which caused two crows to shriek and fly rapidly out of a tree just behind us.

"No we won't be trying to get him to put himself off, just play golf why don't you and let the best man win" He advised shaking his head.

"I don't understand what you mean" I said perplexed "Let the best man win? they are both better than us, do you mean let them win?"

"No just play golf and whoever wins, wins" he said.

"Nope still not getting you Charlie, Walter is out of this match, he's holding every club in a stranglehold and trying to bludgeon the ball to death, all we need to do is to help big Lesley find his inner demon, and job done, we beat two of the best players in the unbearables, happy days and two quid up, what's the problem" I asked genuinely unaware of what his problem could be with my tactics.

"Why not just play them at golf without trying to get some advantage over them with speech play and torture, look at poor

Walter he looks like he's going to set about his golf bag with a nine iron" Charlie asked naively.

I actually giggled "You're winding me up, you're no that daft" I said "Everybody tries to wind up their opponents on a Sunday, it's part of the game, it would be strange if we didnae try it, look at big Lesley I was playing with him a few weeks ago and I was in a bunker, It took me three shots to get out, and when I climbed out of the bunker I said has anybody got a bag of sand I can throw in there, implying obviously that there wasn't enough sand in the bunker, big Lesley answered me, "No but the Conductor has a swing you can borrow", for the rest of that game I wondered what was wrong with my swing and played shite, and that was his intention, so fair play to him it worked"

"Another time when I was playing well and striking it lovely off the tee, he congratulated me on my ability to shape the ball left to right or right to left when I needed it and then asked me on the next tee, what shape I was trying for, just to put doubt in my mind, and it worked again. The bastard, I never hit another decent tee shot all day." I said getting angry at the meories.

"Count me out" he said "I just want to play golf and have a laugh, it shouldn't be about winning a pound"

I nearly fainted who the fuck was this guy I was playing with every week, how could he even joke about it no being about winning, that's if he was joking, he must have been surely, how could anybody think that winning doesn't matter, fuck that for a game of soldiers, winning is the only thing that matters.

But fair enough that meant it was up to me and me alone to win this match, if Charlie wanted to rely on playing better golf that was up to him, but I intended to win, using my head to get inside Lesley's.

"That was a great tee shot on the last hole big man" I said to Lesley "is that wee sway to your left at the top of the backswing to keep the clubface shut through the strike zone" I smiled.

"What wee sway" he asked.

"It disnae matter "I said "it was a great strike anyway"

Charlie and I both hit the green on the fourteenth, Walter topped his ball into the gorse in front of the tee, and Lesley pushed his tee shot to the right, where it landed in some heavy rough behind the bunker.

I smiled at Charlie he shook his head at me, Walter stomped to his bag and Lesley had a few practice swings, clearly concentrating on evenly distributing his weight through the swing.

I whistled as I walked towards the green, Charlie sighed.

We were now two down with four to play, the sun was out and everything was looking up. So of course the best thing for Charlie and me to do was to both hit shite tee shots, he went down the gully to the left of the par three fifteenth and I went into the greenside bunker, bastard bastard.

Lesley smiled at me as he lined up his tee shot and smiled at me again when he hit his six iron to within six feet of the pin, shit, shit, shit.

If we lose this hole we go dormie three down, it was Charlie to play first and he was in the gully, with a very heavy lie, he took an almighty swing at it and got it onto the green about forty feet from the hole.

I swaggered towards the bunker my ball was in and said "Don't forget big man, I'm here in nothing, we're both stroking at this hole" Lesley came over and looked at my ball and grimaced at the lie shaking his head, but I knew his ploy, there was nothing wrong with the lie the ball was lying fine on a gentle up slope nicely on top of the sand, so there's no explanation really as to why when I played my shot the ball hit the lip of the bunker and rolled back down to where it had started, except this time it was in the hole in the sand I had just made, shit, shit, shit.

Walter's tee shot had come up short about ten yards short of the green, so when I was over looking at the line of Charlie's putt it was a slight surprise, when I looked up and saw Walter's ball running across the green gently hitting the flag and falling to the bottom of the hole.

"What was that" I asked, slightly panicky.

"That was Walter's ball, sliding nicely into the hole for a two, Danny boy" was Walter's cheery response, I glanced at Lesley, to be fair he was keeping his laughter under control, just.

I looked in despair at Charlie, he had clearly resigned himself to shaking hands and walked over to his ball and nonchalantly hit it in the general direction of the hole, bear in mind he was forty feet away. I had time to watch Lesley's face and see the amusement drain out of it the nearer Charlie's ball got to the hole, both Lesley and I were on the line of the putt and we could both see the ball veer slightly left away from the hole as it got to within about two feet of the cup, so it came as a complete surprise to both of us when the ball hit a pitch mark, jumped right and fell in the hole for a three net two, hole halved, two down with three to play, we were still in it.

I virtually skipped off the green, Charlie guffawed and Walter and Lesley looked at each other and smiled the smile of the condemned man, they knew it was all over bar the shouting. Both Charlie and I were stroking at the next two holes, and we duly won both of them with a net birdie and a net par, Walter gave us a bit of a fright at the seventeenth, when his par putt circled the hole but just stayed out for a bogie.

"Good match, guys" I said grinning like a fool on the last tee "who would have thought that when we went six down through the first six holes that we would have had any chance of standing on the last hole with a chance to win, you wouldn'y believe it would you, best of luck, eh"

Neither Lesley nor Walter seemed terribly interested in my wee happy speech, strange eh?

I was first to play and hit my seven iron a lovely strike, a really lovely connection and a nice sound, it went almost exactly pin high, but unfortunately for me, thirty yards right of the green and out of bounds. I admired the strength of will it took for all three of them not to laugh in my face.

Charlie knocked his eight iron just through the green not a bad shot in the circumstances, both Walter and Lesley hit sweet nine irons onto the green both about fifteen feet from the hole.

Charlie played a very nice chip which caught the edge of the hole but stayed out and stopped no more than two inches from the cup, he tapped in for his three. Walter played a decent enough putt but came up fractionally short, that left Lesley a fifteen foot putt to win the match.

He asked me a question "How much is in the two's Danny" Bastard, I had forgot about that, there was a hundred and twelve quid in the two's nobody had won it for five weeks.

He lined the putt up and then I swear to god, he pulled his putter back lifted his head and looked at me then completed his putting stroke, he was still looking straight at me and smiling when his ball gently fell into the left and side of the hole. Bastard.

As I went to the bar to order the drinks, the fat controller said, "How did you'se get on, that looked like a good match"

I answered "Walter and Lesley were six up after six holes, but we came back and they only won it with a two on the last hole from big Lesley, so really we can claim the moral victory"

"Claim what you want to claim" he said "but put your moral two quid on the table for the sweep, you lost."

Another match which was worth remembering that summer was the final of the family fourball competition, although it doesn't involve any of the Unbearables except Peter and me, it did provide some thought provoking incidents.

Peter and I had marched quite confidently through the three matches required to reach the family fourball final to find ourselves confronted by twin brothers of obvious Irish descent, the O' Malley's, a couple of very good and extremely consistent golfers.

The format of the match was greensome's, for the uninitiated both golfers drive and then select the best drive, the player who's drive it wasn't then plays the second shot and then alternative shots thereafter.

We won the first hole with a five net four because we were stroking, lost the second hole to a par and halved the third in pars, as I said the O'Malley's were good golfers. Our troubles started at the fourth a short Par three, the O'Malley's teed off and both of them fell short of the green, which theoretically speaking gave us a possible advantage if we hit the green, we didn't.

But to be fair my nine iron shot landed on the fringe of the green in an eminently puttable position, the O'Malley's played their second shot and overshot the green by a few feet in fairly heavy rough, so we were about fifteen feet from the hole in the fringe with an uphill putt in one stroke thanks to my tee shot and they were about forty feet from the hole in rough in two strokes. Easy, just cosy up to the hole and tap in and win the hole, but, Peter decided that as he is a wizard with the wedge he would chip the ball up to the hole, I advised against it.

"It's a simple uphill putt, lag it up to the hole, get it within three feet I'll make the putt they would need to chip in out of the rough to halve the hole" I said

"I know but I'm more comfortable with my wedge from off the green" he answered and played the shot his way, he bladed it twenty feet past the hole into the rough near where the O'Malley's were, not just near them but also behind a bush leaving me a near impossible shot.

I looked at him, he grinned "oops" he said.

"Fuckin oops" I replied trudging to the back of the green with my lob wedge.

The O'Malley's were first to go and bludgeoned the ball out of the rough to about twelve inches from the pin which was a great shot, in the circumstances. I then took my shot and put it about an inch outside theirs, a miraculous shot even if I did say so myself, but like the first three holes the O'Malley's didn't concede the putt, so Peter walked over and nonchalantly one handedly knocked the ball four feet past the cup, I looked away I didn't want to hear him say fuckin oops again.

I knocked the putt in for a five and watched the O'Malley's knock theirs in for a four to go one up in the match, as we walked to the fifth tee I spoke to Peter in a reasonably low voice.

"Concentrate son, that was a five at a short par three when we were sitting 15 feet from the pin in one shot"

He reacted a little huffily "Aye we did take five shots but remember you hit three of them"

I didn't know what to say to that.

At the very next hole Peter put his drive in the trees to the left and I put mine in the light rough at the right side of the fairway leaving about one hundred and forty yards to a narrow green with bunkers to one side and a run off slope to the other.

"It's not a great line in from here" Peter told me "It's a better line to be slightly left of the fairway.

"Where, in the fuckin trees" I asked.

"No need for the angry wee man syndrome to flare up" he says "It's only a game"

"I know it's only a game, but it is a tournament final" I said with what I thought was reasonable calm.

"Aye a tournament with about twenty teams in it, it's hardly the Ryder cup is it, in the first round we beat that wee boy with his Granda, that was his Granda's second game of golf, and his first was during the Falklands war" he answered scathingly.

"for fuck sake it disnae matter how many teams were in it, we have a chance to win it and get our names on a trophy which will be in the trophy cabinet forever, and this is our first year here" I said nudging him towards playing his shot, the O'Malley's were looking over at us from their position in the centre of the fairway.

He moved towards his ball and asked questioningly "Forever?"

"I don't know, probably or for as long as there is a golf club here, or unless there's a nuclear war or we get hit by a comet or a fuckin sunspot or something, gonny play your shot" I replied exasperated.

He selected his seven iron and knocked his shot left of the green left of the bunkers left of the rough and left of the out of bounds fence.

"Oh shit" he said "I was trying to put a bit of left to right on that shot"

"Why?" I asked him dropping a ball to play my next shot.

"Why not?"He answered.

We lost the hole two down.

We again selected my tee shot on the sixth hole, it was marginally better than Peter's, mine was sitting right centre of the fairway about one hundred and eighty yards to the green, his was in a pile of cowshit in the field next to the course.

One hundred and eighty yards to the front of the green, all uphill into a slight to moderate wind.

"Do you think I can get there with a five iron" he asks me.

"Eventually" I reply.

We lost the hole three down.

We halved the next three holes, thanks to the O'Malley's mistakes rather than our brilliance, I think we had bored them into a bad game, by not offering much resistance. Then our luck turned it started raining, heavily.

As we sheltered beneath our umbrellas in the shade of a tree, one of the O'Malley's by this time I had given up caring which one was which, anyway one of them suggested that we postpone for the evening and resume the next night.

"Good idea" I said turning my trolley round and heading for the clubhouse.

"What start again from the first" I heard Peter ask.

"No start from here with the current score" one of them replied "we are three up"

"You canny do that" Peter says "If we cancel it tonight then we start at the first tomorrow all square, or else you'se have an advantage"

"What" the three of us say in unison, me and the O'Malley's.

"It takes me seven or eight holes to get started usually, so I am just about to start playing well, and if we chuck it and just play the back nine tomorrow by the time I get heated up, the match is over, " Peter said indignantly.

That probably made sense to him, we all shook our heads I said "We are pausing the match where it is because of the conditions, it widnae be fair to start again from the first the boys are three up"

"Ok" he said "I get your point, who's on the tee, let's play on"

I looked at him and then looked at the rain, it was torrential, it was bucketing down, there's no way the course would stay open for long.

"Right let's play on" I said, winking at Peter "unless you want to start from scratch tomorrow"

They looked at each other and looked a wee bit annoyed, they walked away and had a quick chat. I think we must have irritated them, because they agreed through gritted teeth to play the next night from the beginning.

I looked at Peter and grinned as he did also. We turned up the next night the weather was perfect the course looked good, Peter had a new Nike driver. We lost six and five. Them O'Malley boys must hold a grudge because when we met them the following year in the semi final they beat us eight and seven, some people take golf too seriously, they should realise it's only a game, It's not just about winning it's about making friends as well, dickheads.

Chapter three; Still Gemme

"Danny, here, that's about the fat controller's sixty fifth birthday party" Jamie McArthur said, handing me an envelope which contained an invitation to the said extravaganza, to be held in the Petersburn bowling club a week from today. The invitation had a picture of an angry golfer bending a putter above his head with both hands, and steam coming out of his ears, a vision I had seen and indeed been more than once, in fact more than once this week.

"It should be a great night wee man, we always have a good swally down at the club, it's a right good laugh as well, and you'll enjoy it" Jamie advised. "Oh but, do yourself a favour and go for something to eat first because the catering has fell through and there might only be crisps and nuts and that"

"Why what happened to the catering" I asked, intrigued.

"Oh it was terrible, it was supposed to be a couple from Bishopbriggs that were doing it, but at a twenty first party two weeks ago, that Bozo, Jasper Lemon ate some of their chicken and got food poisoning" He explained.

"That's no good" I said, sympathetic with Jasper lemon's misfortune.

"Well it was and it wisnae" Jamie continued "It turns out Jasper, wrapped up some of the buffet in napkins and left them in the boot of his car, he then ate them on the way to the golf"

"The next day" I asked, thinking that was a bit dodgy, leaving cooked Chicken in a car boot overnight, no wonder it was off.

"No son, three days later" Jamie answered with his trademark giggle.

"Well how the hell can that be the caterers fault, if he's stupid enough to eat it after three days lying in his car then he's a fuckin eejit and deserves what he gets, surely" I said now more sympathetic to the caterers.

"Well, it wisnae quite as simple as that, when Jasper got a bit no well, it was suggested by Andy that he should contact the caterers and ask them for compensation, they sort of agreed, well they offered two pound a head discount for Andy's sixty fifth, but then last night, there was another do, and somebody mentioned to them that Jasper might have been slightly to blame for his own diarrhoea and told them why."

"Oh definitely not good" I offered my opinion.

"No, not really they phoned Andy's missus and said we were all lying bunch of toe rags and she could look elsewhere for her catering they widnae be doing it, and they would be spreading the word, that we were at it" Jamie said with a grimace "Of course it didn't help that Jasper hidnae told her anything about the food poisoning or the scammed discount. And now it's too late for her to get anybody else" He said laughing.

I didn't really see what was that funny, Andy's poor wife had basically been stitched up by Jasper's stupidity and somehow Jamie and Jasper thought that this was funny?

"How many people is it for" I asked.

"About a hundred and twenty" he replied.

You can ask my wife she would back me up one hundred percent sometimes I open my mouth and say absolutely ridiculous things or make absurdly crazy suggestions.

"Listen Jamie, I've catered a few birthday parties for my family, including my wife's fiftieth which went down really well, if you get all the boys in the winter league to chip in a fiver, I can do it for you" Even as the words left my mouth I knew I had made a major mistake, what the hell was I thinking.

45

His grin was warning enough, "Oh that would be magic wee man, I'll tell his missus, she'll be over the moon, here there's my fiver, I'll collect the rest" he said giggling and scurrying away before I could change my mind.

I looked down at the bundle of change he had put in my hand as "his fiver" there was a total of £3.77 and a plastic ball marker, obviously, the plastic ball marker must have been worth £1.23, to him anyway.

"Oh, by the way wee man, don't say anything to Andy, it's supposed to be a surprise party" he said disappearing through the locker room door.

I went into the smoker's room to find Peter, Charlie and Andy sitting having a coffee.

Andy asked "Are you coming to my party next week wee man"

"What, your surprise sixty fifth birthday party Andy, that party?" I asked in return.

"Aye, that's the one" he said laughing, but clearly not as loudly as Charlie, his guffaw made a waitress drop a tray and even then she made less noise than him.

I was paired that day with Farqhuarson Dixon and Randy Hagen in a three ball. Farqhuarson preferred to be called Sonny for obvious reasons, and didn't take all that kindly to his nickname which was tea bag, this was on account of him being tea total having sworn off the drink some years previously. I had my work cut out for me, as tea bag was on a good run of form and Shagger Hagen was becoming a better player than his da, he could hit the ball for a country mile, although he was a tad temperamental, all you had to do to get his back up was play quite slowly, so I did.

We played a mini points system, which would take at least a chapter to explain so I won't bother, suffice to say Shagger was out of it by the twelfth hole having almost twisted his putter into one of those whirly liquorice sticks, waiting for me to putt at every hole, or waiting for me to select a club when I was in a bunker or on the tee, four times in the first five holes I left my bag at the wrong side of the tee and then just before driving off walked all the way over to my bag and changed my club, twice I actually changed it back again, he wasn't very patient, he seems to have a slight problem with that, he should see somebody, preferably somebody prepared to diagnose him quickly.

Sonny and I were about level, you can't talk Sonny off his game, he has a simple upright stance and a level head, but he does like the sound of his own voice, he is also one of the funniest men on the planet if you measure him by how much he laughs at his own jokes. For example, one of Sonny's often repeated japes which get's funnier every time he does it is to jump behind me whenever anybody shouts fore in our vicinity. He even occasionally shelters behind me when the rain is horizontal. I chuckled along with him the first time, even when he shouted "Quick behind the fat guy" the second time I still chuckled softly, but now that it's been a few years and Happy Valley is a tight course where the shout of fore is a common one, and it rains, a lot, the joke is wearing a wee bit thin. And anyway I'm not fat, it is primarily a height problem that I have, I am far too short for my weight, I should be seven foot two, really.

I happened to mention that I had offered to do some simple catering at Andy's party and they both looked at me as if I was clinically insane.

"You want your head looked at" Shagger said straightforwardly.

"Why?, it's only a wee do in a bowling club, few sandwiches, sausage rolls, some pakora and sauce, bob's your uncle job done, bish bash bosh and all that" I said.

"How many people?" Sonny asked, with a grin that suggested he knew something.

"Jamie McArthur says about a hundred and twenty" I said sceptically.

They both grinned.

"Jamie put out a hundred invitations to his sixty fifth two years ago, two hundred and twenty turned up, somebody head butted the singer in the band, she was in a helluva state, somebody else stole the telly's off the walls in the club and the two lassies that did the catering for the club got a doing because they tried to stop somebody from heating up the sausage rolls by setting fire to a wee pile of paper plates, the toilets in the club were also out of commission for a week because of the amount of napkins people had flushed down them" Shagger seemed to take a particular delight in telling me all this.

Sonny added "I heard that's why the club don't do their own catering anymore and usually don't have private functions anymore, it's probably only because Andy and Jamie are like Jack and Victor from still game down there that they are letting Andy have his party at all"

"What do you mean like Jack and Victor?" I asked starting to see a potential plan.

"Well they are in the middle of everything down there, all the old women hang on their every word and all the old men fall in with whatever them two want, even all the younger boys leave them be, they're well thought of." Shagger said before adding "Personally I think they're a couple of old bawbags, that bring nothing but trouble to the bowling club but nobody asks me. Who the fuck's on the tee this round is taking all fucking day"

It was only because my mind was working flat out devising a way to get out of the problem I had got myself into that Sonny managed to win that day, otherwise I would have beat him comfortably.

I started planning the buffet that very afternoon, I still had a Makro card so I would go out midweek and fill the freezer in the garage with sausage rolls and cold meat and cheese and stuff like that and leave the fresher stuff like bread and rolls to the day before the event. Before I did any of that I fell out with my wife who was supposed to be helping me. I was playing a match on the Wednesday night the week before the party and when I got home I casually mentioned to my wife while she was sitting at the bedroom dressing table plucking her eyebrows "I won tonight"

"Won what" she asked

"My match" I said

"What match" she asked

"My second round match in the singles tournament, Against Francis Boyle" I answered

"Why are you in the singles tournament" she asked

"What do you mean, I am in a few competitions" I innocently asked in return.

I had her full attention now, she stopped plucking and turned round "You are married, why are you in a singles tournament, playing against a woman called Frances"

I laughed gently "Not that kind of single, it's like the opposite of doubles, when you don't have a partner like, and it wasn't a woman it was a guy Francis, you know long for Frank"

"You have got a bloody partner, me" she said missing the point entirely "What are you up to at that happy bloody valley club, are you going about telling people you're single, what is it up there a swinging club or something"

I couldn't help laughing at her saying swinging club, she would be surprised how many people couldn't swing at happy valley.

"Naw don't be daft it just means you play on your own, not with anybody else" I said still amused.

"Do you think I'm completely stupid" she started shouting "Why would anybody play on their own, you could say that you had a hole in one at every hole if you were playing on your own, stop lying to me and you better get them all told at that club that you're married, singles night competition, aye that will be right"

She stood up and grabbed her pyjamas from the pillow on the bed and she pushed past me out of the room. "I'm sleeping in the spare room tonight, then you can practice what it actually is to be single" she slammed the spare room door shut and I heard the lock turn.

I sat down on the edge of the bed, wondering what the fuck had just happened. Then I realised, menopause.

She settled down over the next couple of days and agreed to help at least with the shopping for Andy's party, she still wasn't convinced about my explanation for a singles tournament and vowed to find out more when she met as she put it "Your wee pals at the golf club men and women", give me fuckin strength.

The weekend before the party, Jamie McArthur pulled me into the locker room and put a bundle of cash in my hand it was sixty five quid.

"What the fuck is that" I asked "How do you expect me to feed the multitudes with sixty five quid, Tuna sandwiches?" I thought my reference to loaves and fishes was quite clever it went right over Jamie's head.

"You said, get a fiver each from everybody in the winter league and you would do the rest, I did that's it" he responded pointing to the meagre cash in my hand.

"I thought it would be well over a hundred" I answered.

"Well not everybody's coming" he said "I'm surprised anybody's coming to tell you the truth the wee fat bastard has annoyed everybody at one time or another and made most of them sick as well with them manky sandwiches he brings every week."

I sighed "Right well, since I've already spent more than that, it's more fool me for getting involved I suppose" I then asked "Are you coming down to the club in the morning of the do to help lay all the stuff out or what"

"Naw, it's the monthly medal next week" he said, shocked that I should even ask.

"Well after the medal then, you canny expect me to do everything myself" I said getting riled.

"You offered, and anyway after the medal I will be getting ready for the party" he said.

"What the fuck are you talking about getting ready, look at you the only time you have a wash is when you canny get your umbrella up in time, and I've never seen you without that black cardigan on" I said getting more riled

"That's a bit harsh" he says "when I say getting ready for the party I mean having a few pints in here before I go home, can you no get somebody else to help you?" he asks.

"Naw, I asked you because you're his pal" I said, starting to think of ways to be violent against this old bugger and get away with it.

"Who the hell told you that, I canny stand the fat bastard, I kid on I like him so he well give me one of the manky pieces he brings on a Sunday." He giggled and walked away, as he does frequently.

So that was that then I was on my own, oh well a few sausage rolls and sandwiches for a couple of hundred people what could go wrong.

Actually not much did go wrong, apart from me losing half of my silver trays, well not silver trays but silver coloured metal trays, they were last seen being carried to the bowling club kitchen by the fat controller's nephew. He was going to wash them apparently, maybe he took them home to wash them and is planning on returning them it's only been a few years after all, maybe I shouldn't hold my breath while I wait for their return.

It was generally quite a good night apart from that bozo, Jasper lemon, being a dick on the dance floor, throwing women around with gay abandon or running in circles with somebody else's wife over his shoulder. One of the women he chose to be a dick with was the wife of Pat McGee, this later resulted in a drunken altercation at the back of the bowling club with Jasper and Pat circling each other with fists raised and lashing out with pathetic kicks at each other, if you ever seen any of those bum fights on you tube years ago, it was like that.

It came to nothing, how could it, if either of them had actually ever been able to fight it had been many years ago, or perhaps in another life, it did however leave a bit of an atmosphere between them for a long time. Pat McGee was eventually asked to leave by Andy's wife, after the stramash with Bozo he was going round the hall stirring it up time after time, until eventually Walter Hagen stepped in and manhandled him through the fire exit door. I followed, as I was reasonably sober I had a crazy thought in my head that I should try and help.

"Go home Pat, your making a fool of yourself, you're a bit drunk and being a fanny, I know Bozo is a dick but you knew that before you came, so phone a taxi, get your missus and go home, shake hands with Bozo in the morning, it will all be forgotten about" Walter said trying to calm Pat down, as he was still ranting and raving about Jasper.

"Take my missus home is it Walter, that's a good yin coming from you, who's taking your missus home these day's" Pat slurred.

Walter raised his fist clearly ready to land one on Pat's chin. I grabbed Walter's arm as he pulled it back. "Come on Walter, he's a fanny and he's drunk, it would be taking liberties slapping him, leave it be come in and sit with your fiancée, I'll put him in a taxi, come on inside fuck him he's an idiot" I said manhandling him gently through the door back into the club. I looked over my shoulder and said "Pat fuck off home pal, that's two people who want to punch you, if you don't beat it I will make it three except I'll no miss, now fuck off, before you start anything else"

"Ah'm no shrunk Dinny" Walter said.

"I know you're no drunk Walter, I was just saying that to get rid of him. Come on sit down at your table and I'll get you a pint" I said chuckling.

I sat him next to his fiancée Lesley, she is a gorgeous lovely young blonde with luscious lips, eyes that sparkle with humour and raw sex appeal, a body to die for. I do not have a Scooby doo what she was doing with Walter, I can only imagine he was blackmailing her in some way, poor sweet girl.

Walter's son Randy came over to ask what the problem was, with Pat McGee, I reassured him there was no problem that Pat was just being a fanny and Walter had put his gas at a peep.

"I didnae like him, that Pat McGee, I felt as if he was undressing me with his eyes all night" Lesley said with the voice of an angel, a Glaswegian angel at that.

That was enough to have both Shagger and Walter race out of the fire exit after Pat McGee, fortunately they were too late he was long gone.

Randy came up to me and said "I'm going to do that Pat McGee in one of these days" he looked over his shoulder to make sure his father wasn't listening and said "It might have been him that split my ma and up you know Danny, he's lucky my Da didnae kill him, one of these days I might just whack a five iron over his head, the fanny"

"Ok, ok Shagger take it easy" I said, go back over and sit with them two lovely wee lassies, you're in there.

Shagger laughed and said "No you've got the wrong end of the stick wee man roll your tongue in, my girlfriend's on holiday in Magaluf this week, and I'm the faithful type, they two wee lassies you are talking about are into each other I'm just sitting have a laugh with them"

The remainder of the night thankfully passed without any more violence, although there was a fair amount of drunkenness and a small amount of debauchery. The drunkenness was mainly around Andy Ingles, Jamie McArthur and Bozo, to be fair to Andy and Jamie neither of them vomited in the corner of the hall or pished down the front of their trousers, both of those incidents were Jasper Lemon, no wonder he is nicknamed Bozo.

While my wife and me were waiting for a taxi and she was taking pains to explain to me the many ways that Jasper Lemon was a fuckwit. I was approached by one of Andy's nephews.

"Are you Danny" he asked glancing both ways and over his shoulder as he approached me, presumably looking to make sure no one was within earshot.

"Aye" I said looking him up and down "Who are you and do you think somebody's following you or something, is it the police, your awfully nervous" I answered, also looking both ways and glancing over both of my shoulders.

"Well, half of the people you play golf with are police, I canny believe my uncle Andy brought them to the club I thought it was a fuckin raid at first, I recognised that one Baxter Carter, I'm sure he nicked me once the baldy old bastard and wouldn'y even let me go when I offered him a monkey" he said.

"Where did you get a monkey" my wife asked him. "That's cruel"

"He means £500, he's been watching too much Eastenders hen" I said, Patricia, my missus then wandered over to talk to Lesley Clifford's wife who was slightly worse for wear but still able to stand, just.

"What do you want son" I asked Andy's nephew who it turns out was also called Danny.

"Nothing really, just to say this was good of you and to maybe offer you a wee deal" He said again glancing sideways watching his back.

"If you mean drugs son, you can get to fuck, do I look like a cracked head" I said getting riled.

"Naw, naw big man calm down, why would I offer drugs to a gentleman like you, naw, I'm offering you a wee deal on transport" he said with a grin.

"Transport?" I asked bewildered "do you mean a motor?"

"Naw, a mobility scooter" He said his grin getting wider.

I looked at my stomach and then at him "Are you trying to be funny or is it a slap you're after, I might be getting a bit of a belly on me son, but I don't need a fuckin mobility scooter wee man." I said moving towards him slightly.

"Calm down big chap, fuck sake, my uncle Andy's right about you, you have got wee angry man syndrome, I've got a haud of two mobility scooters, a pal of mine has adapted them so that they can carry golf clubs on the back of them and I'm trying to flog them, my uncle Andy said you had a few bob and might buy them and sell them on to some of the old boys at the club, what do you think?" he said moving from foot to foot and looking like the lassie in the exorcist he was trying to swivel his head round that much.

"Why are you so jumpy," I asked also looking round to try and see what was making him twitchy.

"These two mobility scooters" he says "Just by sheer coincidence look a bit like two mobility scooters that went missing from this very bowling club a few weeks ago, and I don't want anybody putting two and two together and getting four, know what I mean?, in fact that's the two people they belonged to"

He pointed at an elderly man and an even more elderly old woman who were both being carried piggy back style out to a taxi by what I suppose where their grandchildren.

"For Christ's sake son, have you no got a conscience, give them their scooters back, look at them, they need to be carried to a taxi." I said appalled.

"Naw, don't worry about them big man, they are insured, and anyway they get carried out every week whether they have their scooters or no, they're both absolutely steaming and widnae be safe to drive a scooter, anyway when I sell these scooters they will get a ton each for their trouble, everyone's a winner eh big man" he said laughing softly.

"How much?" I asked "how much each and how much if I take both of them?" I had started thinking this could work, not that I would sell them to the old boys at the club, but I could part sell them to Stan and Oliver the club professionals, and they could hire them out, give me a cut on every hire, and happy days, there could be a few quid in this if I play my cards right.

He put on his shifty act again, swaying as he spoke "Well, they retail at £1200 but I could probably let you have them for £500 each"

"They retail for £1200, do you think you're on dragons den for fuck sake" I said "I'll come and have a look at the tomorrow and then I will let you know, fucking retail at £1200" I said as I turned and walked towards my wife, our taxi had arrived.

"Aw big man wait a minute the thing is I need the money the night," young Danny said holding my arm.

"Who is that you think is stupid son, me or you. I suppose it must be me, aye your right wait a minute I think I've got a grand in my pocket, I'll just hand it over to you and see you tomorrow about your imaginary scooters, eh, piss off son" I said getting into the back seat of the car beside my wife.

Young Danny hopped into the front seat of the car beside the driver and said, "Haw driver take us down to Broomfield road next to Springburn Park will you" He turned to Patricia and said "I've got a wee bit of business with your man doll it will only take ten minutes, its cool"

Patricia answered him "It's not cool, it's fuckin freezing' and you want to go to a park, are you mental?"

It was against my better judgement and I knew it would lead to trouble, but we did go and have a look at the scooters. All the way there Danny regaled me with tales of how much of an honest and upstanding citizen he was and how it was only a temporary cash flow problem that had forced him into a life of petty crime, and how when he made it big, which he would, any day now, he wouldn't be forgetting the people who helped him on his rollercoaster journey through the hard streets of Glasgow, this eejit watched far too much X-factor, I thought.

We got there in less than twenty minutes, and the scooters where in front of us three minutes after that.

"I suppose they look alright" I said "Even though the new bit welded on to the back to carry the clubs, isnae that great is it?"

Young Danny answered in full salesman mode "Well that's bespoke welding that, I think maybe he was trying to give it a nostalgic Glesga feel, like shipyards and cranes and aw that"

"What?" I asked "What are you wittering about, it's meant to hold a golf bag, not lift the Queen Mary out of the clyde" I inspected it more closely and said "The welding is quite ugly but I suppose a tin of metallic paint would hide the worst bits"

"Ah big man now you're thinking outside the box I like it, I can see where you're going there" Danny enthused.

"Gonny shut the fuck up son, you're getting on my nerves now with that shite, you're not Duncan Bannatyne, or even Duncan Doughnut's" Patricia said to him, by now bored and cold and busy trying to get her stiletto heel out of the patch of grass she was standing on, she had actually told me once that she thought Duncan Doughnuts was the name of the guy who invented doughnuts, straight up.

"I'm not giving you £500 each for them, I might give you £500 for the pair and anyway I'm not giving you anything until I get somebody to look at them and check them over" I said and turned to my wife. "Phone a taxi Trish will you hen"

"Haw big man come on now, you know I'm a wee bit desperate for cash the night, so I don't blame you for trying to mug me, fair doos and that, but I'll tell you what, take them as seen and I will pop them on to that trailer in my uncles garage, bung me an extra twenty and we'll drive them over to your bit, shake on it" he said spitting on his hand and holding it towards me.

I looked at him with disgust on my face and said "Do you think my head buttons up the back wee man, I told you until I get somebody to check them out and make sure they're running no cash changes hand comprehende"

Just as I turned and motioned to Patricia that the business was over and it was time to go, I heard a voice behind me.

"We will make sure they work Danny, no problem" Andy Ingles and Jamie McArthur had appeared from nowhere and they were now both sitting on a mobility scooter each, trying to work out how to start them.

"You need a key numpty" young Danny said to Jamie, at the same time taking two keys from his pocket and handing them one each. Both scooters started up instantly and they were pretty soon humming along Broomfield road and into Springburn Park.

"See big man, good as new, look at them two go, I'm reluctant to let them go for £500 now, they are worth at least that each" Danny said rubbing his hands together.

They did appear to be running very smoothly and I was thinking this could be a very lucky night, but I wasn't stupid enough to rub my hands together, yet.

Danny Patricia and me, wandered over to the park fence and watched Andy and Jamie racing each other along the paths, at one point both of them had their hands in the air shouting "Look ma no hands".

Patricia pointed into the park and asked young Danny "What's that dark patch them two are heading straight for"

Young Danny shook his head and hung it down "That would be the fuckin boating pond missus, fuckin arseholes" he shook his head again and said "I'll phone you a taxi big man, you better get your good lady hame she looks freezing"

We all heard the almighty splash and the screams that followed as we walked up to the main road to wait for a taxi. Fanny's.

Chapter four; look out Ayrshire here we come

"Da, have you noticed there's a bit of animosity towards Pat McGee, the guy that runs this winter league" Peter asked me, as we drove down to play the course at Prestwick St Nicholas, the first leg of our three day golf outing in the heart of Ayrshire.

We were scheduled to play Prestwick on day one, loch green on day two and Dundonald links on day three, we had two nights full board at a decent quality hotel, a bargain at less than two hundred quid a head, well I thought it was a bargain anyway.

"I canny really say I've noticed Peter, I have seen a few people doubting his arithmetic skills, he seems to get a five mixed up with a six quite a lot, but I canny say I've seen any animosity, no really" I replied, but now that he had put that thought in my head there had been a few mumblings of con man and rip off artist, things like that.

"Aye one or two of the guys have been doing a fair bit of moaning about the cost of this and the cost of that, I think some of them think he's at it you know" Peter said clearly expecting a response from me. "If he is at it, I wouldn'y mind organising the society, I could do a spread sheet for keeping the scores and a website, it would be a dawdle"

"Well our problem is we have only been here a few months so we don't know what might be behind this, what history there might be, if you know what I mean. The best thing is for us to stay out of it especially, if anything kicks off, we should definitely stay out of it" I replied. "But if he is a rogue and nobody else wants to do it then do it, but get somebody else to handle any money because that's what always causes the trouble, stay away from the cash and it's not a big deal"

"Aye, which sounds exactly like you Da, I'm actually looking forward to hearing you say, it's nothing to do with me, and I'm saying nothing." Peter said smiling at me "Never gonny happen, I'll give it twenty minutes before you start shouting and bawling and calling somebody a fanny"

"Well just wait and see I'm a reformed angry wee man, I hardly ever call anybody a fanny any more, much" I told him, just as a white van overtook me on the inside and I chased him for three miles so I could tell him very loudly that he was driving like a fanny. Well he was.

A roll and bacon and a cup of strong coffee, an ideal culinary delight before starting a round of golf, sounded good to me, anyway. We had hardly settled down at our table before the moaning started.

"Why is this no included in the price of our golf Pat" This was a question posed to Pat McGee by David Simpson, nicknamed the part timer due to his tendency to walk off the course if he wasn't playing particularly well, although to be fair he has improved he sometimes lasts to the sixth hole now.

"Aye you would think that at the price we are paying they could throw in a coffee and a bacon roll" Agreed Billy Paterson "It's a bit much having to pay extra for weak coffee and cold bacon" he added.

Pat McGee looked a little aggravated, "I never even asked when I was booking it, I didnae think" was his muttered response. "Can we stop moaning about a couple of quid for a minute and get the rest of this done, I need twenty quid each for the daily sweeps and the two's competitions"

"You must be joking, was that no included in the total either, what are you up to" asked Igor Currie looking directly at Pat McGee. Igor is a big lad, maybe six feet or more and almost as broad as he is tall, hence the affectionate nickname chubby, or maybe it's because he likes playing draughts. (a joke for the oldies)

"Hold on a minute guys, we are here to play golf, if it's another twenty quid then it's another twenty quid, this is getting a bit heavy, let's get the draw done and have a game of golf before it gets dark" I said, not my best ever joke, but it was enough to make Charlie guffaw which broke the ice a bit.

There was still a certain amount of mumbling, well outright mutiny would describe it better than mumbling, but everyone paid up and eventually the draw was started, Pat McGee was drawn out with David Simpson, Igor Currie and Billy Paterson, probably the three people who mistrusted him the most, that's not to say that everybody else trusted him, far from it.

I was drawn to play with Rob Chandler, the talkative septuagenarian Geordie, a lovely man who clearly adored the sound of a Geordie accent, Jason McKechnie, the quiet man and Harry Caravan nicknamed the snail. I had played with all three previously and all three of them are good company on a golf course.

As long as you take care to time your swings to coincide with the Geordies pauses for breath, teach Harry to walk and talk at the same time, and listen carefully to Jason he doesn't say much but is very droll when he does, and it's usually worth hearing. I remember the day I played with him and he had his first ever hole in one at age eighty, a five iron hit into the wind at a hundred and forty two yard downhill par three, he hit it sweetly it went straight at the pin, took one hop, tracked slightly left to right and hesitated on the lip and fell in, sheer joy on the tee.

Three golfers including me jumped in the air with howls of "It's in, get in there, ya beauty" Jason turned to us and said "I think I caught that a wee bit fat, I nearly missed it"

We had been lucky with the weather this year for late April it was unseasonably warm, which meant I got the chance to wear my new tartan golf shorts, which in my opinion were the height of sophistication when it came to golfing attire, bizarrely nobody shared my opinion. I had intended to wear my YES Scotland polo shirt, but Peter had convinced me that as much as I liked fighting and being condescending about the independence referendum, everybody else would appreciate a break from my bullshit, apparently.

"What the fuck is that you've got on did somebody sew up the middle of your kilt fat boy" This came from bozo, it was his way of saying "good morning Danny how are you" Jamie McArthur giggled and scurried past Charlie guffawed and asked if my shorts constituted a breach of the peace, Andy Ingles broke into a chorus of "Danny where's your trousers" Fanny's the lot of them.

Prestwick St Nicholas is a lovely golf course and the weather on the day made it even better, the fourball I played with all played reasonably well particularly Jason McKechnie who finished with 38 points, a good score in terms of the Stableford scoring system and should have put him in second place on the day it didn't because Jason marked down a score of five on his card when in fact he had had a four.

A simple mistake that actually made his score worse than it should have been, this caused a bit of a row in the clubhouse after the game, when Pat McGee insisted that Jason needed to be disqualified ,which coincidentally left him in second place with 37 points.

"The rules are the rules, or do we just not bother with rules, you need to put your scores down correctly or the whole things is a waste of time" Pat McGee was pontificating to all around him, he was basically under siege to a man everyone else in the room defended Jason and told Pat not to be a ridiculous fanny.

"If we start disqualifying people for not counting up properly, you would be out on your arse every bloody week" Igor Currie said to Pat.

"What's that supposed to mean, my scorecard is always correct and always signed, and I'll not be getting disqualified." Pat spat back angrily.

Billy Paterson jumped in on Igor's side and added angrily "Aye your scorecard's only right because people point out your counting mistakes before you write them down and it's never a mistake where you write a higher number down than it should be, that's no the kind of mistakes you make"

"Are you saying I'm a cheat or something" Pat McGee said getting to his feet.

"If the baseball cap fit's then wear it" I heard someone behind me whisper, it might have been bozo or the fat controller, they were both sat at the table directly behind me.

I put in my tuppence worth "Can we just calm down a minute, this is getting nasty. The point is Jason made a daft wee mistake it's no harm done, it's a golf outing for fucks sake not the Augusta

Master's, put his 38 points in give him his second prize it's only a sleeve of golf balls and let's go and get some dinner."

Pat McGee looked as if he wanted to say something but a quick glance round put him off from raising any objection, although he did mumble almost inaudibly "OK no rules then"

The surprise came when Jason himself walked to Pat's table picked up his scorecard, ripped it in half and dropped it in a bin and said "There will be no more arguing because I'm a stupid old sod that canny count" and walked out of the room towards the locker rooms.

I turned to Pat McGee and said "You really can be a fanny, there was no need for that" and followed Jason out, I heard Bozo say to Andy "oops our great leader has upset wee fat Danny, wait till he hears Pat's voting NO in the referendum as well, that will really piss him off" which raised a few sniggers but the atmosphere was such that nobody felt much like laughing.

We all gathered in the hotel dining room for our evening meal where the mood was rather quiet and subdued, Pat McGee was oblivious to the atmosphere and merrily announced the four balls for the next day which he had drawn in his hotel room.

"You really are a thick skinned dickhead aren't you" Billy Paterson said to Pat.

"Why what have I done now" Pat asked looking round in bewilderment.

"Jason's having something to eat in his room, he say's a bit tired tonight" Barney Piper said. Barney Piper was normally an ebullient big guy, happy go lucky and up for a laugh, I hadn't seen him this upset before. Well not since Glasgow Rangers died anyway.

"What you did now, was that you deliberately embarrassed one of the nicest guys in this society, just so you could win a sleeve of golf balls, you're a dickhead, end of story" Barney added stood up and left the dining room, adding as he went "I'm away for a curry, it stinks in here" Several of the other golfers rose and followed him out, almost to a man they dropped their napkins on the table in front of Pat McGee.

Andy Ingles commented, "A curry sounds good but I've paid for this meal, but then again I don't want to be seen as siding with Pat, because he has been a dickhead, it's quite a dilemma, fuck it, I'm going for a curry as well."

This was the cue for Jamie McArthur and the two Hagen's to follow him out although Jamie did fill his pockets with bread rolls as he went. I have no idea why, maybe hewas going to feed the pigeons on the way to the Indian. This left Peter Charlie and I sat at one table and Pat McGee sat at another.

"So what do we do Da, are you up for a curry" Peter asked.

Charlie said "I am" and stood.

I hesitated, this was getting a bit out of hand, sure McGee was out of order but totally isolating him felt wrong, he hadn't even been given a chance to apologise perhaps he would if given the chance.

Pat then said "What the fuck's the matter with all them, Jason put the wrong score down, what was I supposed to do just ignore it?"

I stood up and said "A chicken Bhuna Masala sounds just the thing, get a move on or Bart Cooper will have drunk all the Cobra before we get there."

I glanced over my shoulder, Pat McGee was consulting the menu, seemingly oblivious to his isolation, and I almost had a sympathetic thought, almost.

The owners of the Indian Restaurant were over the moon, twenty odd fat hungry golfers, Bari Khusi. I was almost correct, the restaurant ran out of Cobra beer ten minutes after we arrived, an S, O, S was put out to other restaurants in the area to get new supplies in pronto. We drank all of that as well, I say we, I mean they.

It was a buffet night so for £10.99 it was "all you can eat" that was a mistake, we were there for three hours, and we have a double handful of world class greedy bastards and a smattering of ordinary greedy bastards. The only consolation for the owners was the bar bill, which would have lifted more than one African country out of poverty.

There were differing levels of drunkenness, ranging from Sonny Dixon's complete sobriety to Bart Coopers self induced coma, which he entered at approximately 10.30 pm, but miraculously emerged from at about two in the morning, only to start drinking again as soon as he opened his eyes.

The majority of the guys headed back to the Hotel between eleven o'clock and midnight, a select few predominantly the younger ones headed for a late night bar come night club. bear in mind when I say the young ones I mean people in their thirties, forties and fifties. The Unbearables don't do young, the consolation is that in twenty years they will presumably be extinct.

Young Shagger Hagen the exception to the no youngsters rule, had the girls swarming around him again, probably because of his excellent physique and his myriad of tattoos which promoted his macho image, a little bit spoiled by his cheap copy of a Hugo Boss watch and his cartoon character belt. Anyway young Shagger is an extremely faithful young Christian boy and only engaged these young scantily clad girls in conversation as an intellectual diversion from his religious studies. I would imagine it was a religious studies group that the two girls who left his room at seven the next morning had been attending, amen.

A few of the middle aged Lothario's had to be ejected by the security team at the nightclub, when they lost the ability to roll their tongues back into their heads, as well as the ability to walk and talk simultaneously, why do drunk people need to stand still and hold on to your arm in order to have a conversation? Actually on that basis I wonder if Harry Caravan is drunk every Sunday morning.

I was actually tucked up by one am, having tried in vain for two hours to teach Jamie McArthur to play poker.

"Two pair, beats one pair, Jamie" I said getting exasperated.

"No but, your got a pair of threes and a pair of two's that adds up to a pair of fives and I've got a pair of seven's I won you wee bastard you're cheating me" He replied.

I sighed "You won what numbnuts, I'm only showing you what hand beats what other hands, we aren't playing for anything yet" I half shouted at him, on theory that perhaps he was deaf rather than completely stupid" He isn't deaf.

"You're just telling me things that will let you take money off me later, you can make up any rules you want and then skin me later on" he slurred.

"Jamie, I was sitting here quite happily teaching Sonny Dixon the basics of poker, you came and sat down beside us and slur, mumbled "show me tay." I'm showing you tay and you think I'm cheating so as I can rob you later, I've got a good idea" I said and hesitated.

"What good idea" he slurred.

"Fuck off" I advised

"There's no need for that you wee bastard, I was just being sociable" he said grinning his unrelenting grin and giggling his trademark giggle.

"You're right Jamie, I should be more polite, so why don't you please fuck off, thank you" I further advised.

Andy Ingles joined us "Are you stealing all of this stupit bastards money Danny" he asked sociably.

"Aye Andy, do you want dealt in" I asked.

"OK" he responded.

After a few minutes of attempting to teach them the basics of poker, which was actually pretty similar to trying to putt with a piece of rope, I gave up and taught them how to play shoot, a relatively simple children's game where everybody is dealt three cards and the object of the game is to gamble whether one of your cards is of the same suit but of a higher value than a random card turned over by the dealer. It took them half an hour to get the basics. A long fuckin half an hour at that.

We played for money for a couple of hours, the big winner on the night was Andy Ingles. He walked away with the majority of the chips which was mildly surprising on two levels, firstly he stopped actually playing after ten minutes. And secondly Jamie McArthur had the luck of the devil and won almost every hand he played, so it was surprising that when the chips were cashed in Andy had most of them. It may have been because every time Jamie McArthur's eyes closed for a nano second due to the combination of him being drunk, tired and ancient, Andy Ingles purloined his stack of chips. When I chastised Andy about this, he claimed that he and Jamie had that kind of friendship and it was none of my business. Fair enough, everybody needs friends.

I think it was probably about eight o'clock when I went down to breakfast, leaving Peter, whom I was sharing a room with lying bollock naked on the floor beside his bed, just as well we are related. I had heard him come in at roughly three o'clock and was reluctant to wake him now for breakfast, I threw a cover over him to save him any embarrassment when the chamber maids came to change the towels. I needn't have bothered I later found out that he had indeed came into the room at three but having got up to go to the toilet he had walked out of the room and pished in a plant pot holding a rubber plant in the corridor outside our door.

He apparently then, still bollock naked, attempted to enter four doors in the corridor none of which was our room, he was guided back to our room and let in by the night porter who had found him in the reception area trying to find someone who could remind him where his room was, still bollock naked mind you. Sometimes parental pride can be overwhelming and bring a tear to your eye, other times not so much.

Amazingly Bart Cooper was already at breakfast, this was extremely astonishing, I had last seen him at about three o'clock being carried out of the hotel bar by four of our members each one grasping a limb, yet here he was nice as ninepence sitting tucking into a full English, well actually a full Scottish because of the lovely wee slice of haggis.

"No way Bart, you can't actually be sitting here, I thought you were probably gonny be dead this morning, you were utterly and completely out of it just a few hours ago" I said sitting down beside him.

"I wisnae that bad," he says. "Nothing a wee fried breakfast canny fix"

I shook my head in wonder and went to the buffet part of the breakfast spread. When I returned to the table with a plate of fresh fruit and a croissant Bart took a look and said "What is that your having" he paused to wipe the brown sauce of his top lip and continued "Fruit and cakes for your breakfast, you'll make yourself ill"

Just at that a waitress approached and asked us if we would like a drink, I ordered coffee, Bart declined saying he had already ordered and on cue a second waitress arrived with Bart's order, a pint of cold Guinness.

"Aye your right thanks for the advice Bart" I said "all this fruit and pastry is probably gonny make me ill in the long run" He smiled at the waitress burped and said "No problem Danny just looking out for you pal"

Time to play golf, our second venue was loch green a municipal golf course in Troon, a very nice course with a mixture of parkland and links holes, something to look forward to, (you would think).

We assembled in the clubhouse bar at loch green to be allocated our scorecards and determine the order of play, there was still an undercurrent of tension between several people and Pat McGee. Jason McKechnie did his best to remove the tension by being civil to Pat when he arrived he said good morning and sat down waiting for his card the same as everybody else. So by following his lead we were all able to get on with the days golf without harping back to the previous days situation. There were of course various barbed comments and whispered uttering's regarding Jason's mistreatment by Pat but nothing vitriolic or vicious, much.

My fourball that day included Charlie, David Simpson and Pat McGee, whoopee. Neither Charlie or I had much time for Pat but couldn't be arsed joining in a vendetta against him, David on the other hand disliked him intensely and made it quite clear by word and deed that he felt that way.

It was a bad tempered round of golf with David consistently sniping at Pat. Charlie and I consistently looking at each other and alternatively shrugging our shoulders or shaking our heads. It didn't particularly damage our scoring Charlie had a good solid 38 points and I managed a lucky two at the designated hole to win the two's money for the day a handy £50. Pat was more or less oblivious to David's sniping and managed another 37 points as he had on the first day, we later learned in the club house that this put Pat in the lead, to just about everyone's disappointment.

The unhappiness about pat being in the lead multiplied when Jason finished his round with 38 points again, which would have put him in the lead had his first round score stood. Surprisingly it was Billy Paterson and Igor Currie who brought the subject up again when we were all sitting in the Loch green clubhouse having a pint and preparing to head back to the hotel.

Billy stood up and hit the side of his pint tumbler with a parker pen; "Can I have some hush, a few of us" he indicated Barney, Igor and David "Have had a wee talk and we want to propose that we have an egm, tonight at the hotel"

Jamie McArthur whispered to me "What's an egm"

I answered him "It's like an egg and spoon race but with no eggs and no spoons"

He looked bewilderedly at me and Andy poked him in the back and said "It's a meeting of the unbearables golf society, for all of us, egm stands for extraordinary general meeting, instead of the annual general meeting which is an agm"

Jamie turned back to me and said "What's that got to do with eggs and spoons then"

Andy said "for fucks sake" and sat back and finished his pint in one swallow.

As no objections were raised it was agreed to have a meeting with everybody in attendance at six forty five meaning we had forty five minutes to say our piece before we had to sit down to dinner, one small objection was made, it was by Pat McGee.

"As long as this meeting isn't Danny's idea and he uses it to make us all vote aye" he said grinning like a buffoon. It raised a couple of titters but I don't think he realised that he was about to be deposed, everybody else had worked that out already he hadn't, fanny.

"Do we need this shit" Peter asked me, as we sat at a table with Bart Cooper the Hagen's Sonny Dixon, and Lesley Clifford also joined us.

"No we certainly don't" answered Bart, "It's better to let sleeping dogs fart"

Walter agreed "Aye just reinstate wee Jason's score, and get on with it, who gives a shit if Pat's a dickhead we know he is anyway, so what's the big deal, fuckin growing up is what they need to do."

The young Hagen didn't venture an opinion he was completely focussed on trying to angle his chair in the direction of three young lassies on the other side of the room, he was twisting and turning trying to make sure they could get the best view possible of him, he flexed his tattoos and smoothed his mohican.

Lesley and I both agreed that this was not going to be pleasant there could be harsh words said, words that quite possibly couldn't be taken back and indeed words that could and probably would lead to violence. Andy Ingles overheard us and immediately started a book on who would hit McGee first, the only proviso being that you couldn't bet on yourself, he abandoned the idea when he heard me asking Peter to thump McGee the second he walked through the door because I had two quid on him to do so, It didn't help when Walter told Shagger to do the same thing.

Eventually everyone assembled grouped around four separate tables, the only one I couldn't see was old Jack Sharp. It's a fair guess he was away having a pish.

Pat McGee stood up "Ladies and gentlemen, although there isnae any ladies or gentlemen here, can I have your attention. It was agreed today that we would hold an egm, before we open the egm can I just say one thing, the incident with Jason yesterday was probably down to me so I think I might have been a bit harsh, he is an old yin after all"

This was said presumably slightly tongue in cheek, I don't think Jason entirely saw it that way.

Pat continued after seeing Jason scowl "That was just a week joke Jason, anyway, what I propose is that we take Jason's score from yesterday and reinstate it. Get on with our dinner and have a good night out and then a good days golf tomorrow, does anybody second that proposal"

There were a few ayes and a general murmur of agreement until Igor Currie stood up and said "Haud on a minute, you canny make a proposal and ask for seconders before the meetings even opened"

Jack Sharp having re-entered the room while drying his hands on the remains of a paper towel said "Hey Danny, I thought you were the councillor no Igor"

This got a general laugh but Billy Paterson jumped to his feet in support of Igor "Big Chubby's right" he said not noticing Igor's less than enthusiastic reaction to his nickname. "This meeting isnae only about what happened to Jason yesterday, It's more serious than that, it's about being taken for a ride and having our pockets dipped, it's about thieving actually"

Igor stood up again and said "As the meetings now opened David Simpson has something to tell you'se aw"

David stood up looking slightly ill at ease, "Well it's like this I got chatting to one of the lassies in reception last night just before we all went out" A few wolf whistles and cries of "confession time" broke out, David smiled awkwardly and continued the thing is she told me what the hotel rates are and what was paid for our golf package, she said it was £170.00 a head, well as far as I can remember Pat charged all of us £190.00 a head, so I was sort of

77

wondering whether Pat wanted to let us know what happened to the extra twenty quid"

The room silenced you could have heard a contact lens land on the carpet, then a low level buzz swept round the room as a few people spoke in a whisper to whoever they were sat beside. I noticed an angry Barry Monk, wee Hawkeye, make angry gestures with his hands as he spoke to The Mad Geordie and Jason McKechnie, all three of them started to become slightly animated as did Jack Sharp who sat with them.

Bozo Jasper Lemon, turned to Andy and asked, "Does that mean we have to pay an extra twenty quid then"

Andy answered him the only way you would expect "No, you fanny, that means that he owes all of us twenty quid, he's overcharged us hopefully by mistake"

David Simpson overheard this last remark and corrected Andy "No Andy it's not a mistake, the lassie showed me the actual invoice that got sent to him, he knows full well what the price is"

"Come on now" I said "Maybe the twenty quid was for prize money or something or maybe there's an extra charge that lassie isnae know about or something, it's a bit early to be accusing anybody of anything"

Pat McGee looked flustered but grabbed the lifeline that I had inadvertently offered him.

"Aye there was a surcharge of twenty quid a head, I've not got the invoice with me but I will find it, and bring it next Sunday" he stammered, it was clear to everyone there that he was hiding something, perhaps he was, perhaps he wasn't we might well never know.

Igor Currie stood and quite brutally said "You're a liar, you've pocketed that cash, probably to pay for your own outing"

"Well actually that's no true either," young Shagger Hagen popped in to the conversation.

"After Davie spoke to that lassie last night I got talking to her just as she finished her shift, anyway to cut a long story short she came up to my room for a wee while and happened to mention that if you book more than twenty people the organiser goes free" young Shagger looked a little embarrassed about being involved, he shrugged his shoulders and sat down.

Again playing devil's advocate, I butted in "Maybe he's entitled to go free he does seem to do a fair bit of organising."

Billy Paterson answered me "You're right, he does do a fair bit and is probably entitled but why hide it and what's the extra twenty quid a head for that's nearly £500, that's a fair amount of money. I widnae mind £500 in my sky rocket"

He had made a very good point and all I could offer was that the extra twenty quid a head hadn't been proven, but I along with everyone else in the room knew that it had, just by Pat McGee's blustering attitude.

Pat stood up and gathered his papers and attempted to make light of the matter and escape unscathed, "Some people might owe me an apology next week when I turn up with that invoice for the surcharge eh?" he scurried out of the room.

Barney Piper said loud enough for Pat to hear "And some people might owe you a kick in the baws if you don't"

I looked at Peter and Charlie and shook my head, if this incident reduces one of the good guys like Barney to threats, what was to become of the unbearables if we didn't get rid of McGee.

The meeting broke up and everyone drifted away in different directions, I spoke to various of the guys and the consensus seemed to be that Pat had been caught with his fingers in the cookie jar and should pay everybody back and resign, not just from the Unbearables but from the golf club altogether. I argued that it seemed a bit harsh, it could yet turn out to be a mistake and even if Pat was making a wee skin, was it the end of the world, just tell him he wasn't handling any cash anymore, the shame would probably be punishment enough.

Understandably there was major opposition to my suggestion, primarily that we were, if not exactly his friends, we did all play golf together each week and if he did scam us out of money that was equivalent to going through our pockets in the locker room. I didn't agree with that analogy then and I still don't to this day. We will never know the truth because of what happened that night, but I refuse to tar and feather anybody without sufficient evidence.

As Peter and I wandered down to the dining room a bit later, it was only Pat McGee who was sat in there. "Let's go down to the Indian's Da, everybody else must be down there tonight again" Peter advised, trying perhaps to dodge out before Pat spotted us.

"Aye in a minute, let me have a word with Pat first" I said, winking at him in an attempt to assuage his fears, on past performance peter may have thought I intended to have it out with Pat, the opposite is true. This situation was awful, I enjoyed playing golf, I enjoyed playing at Happy Valley, I enjoyed playing with the unbearables, but I defy anyone to enjoy playing golf under these circumstances.

"How goes it Pat" I asked sitting opposite him at a table meant to seat ten people.

"All right Danny, just sitting sorting out some stuff for the final round tomorrow, now that Jason is reinstated from Friday he's in the lead, but anybody can still win it, what do you think?" he asked. I don't know if Pat was really this oblivious to everything that had been said earlier in the day or he was just trying to keep up appearances, but it came across as a little odd.

"Pat, I don't think anybody can be arsed playing golf tomorrow to be honest, you need to give them some answers, did you have a wee fiddle going, because if you did then man up tell them it was to cover all the time you put in doing all the organising for just about everything, and if they want the somebody else then you will stand aside and let them do it." I advised.

Pat got angry, apologetic and angry again he began by raising his voice and saying "You have got no right accusing me of fiddling the books, who do you think you are, you've only been here five minutes?" then added "Sorry, I'm just scunnered with all the work I put in, I don't see half of them getting off their fat arses and helping, if it wisnae for me they widnae even have the Unbearables, lazy bastards most of them"

"So tell them that it wisnae a fiddle it was to cover your time and they can like it or lump it." I further advised. "Just tell the truth and it will blow over"

He got angrier "I never said that, I haven't touched a penny of anybody's money, it's been a mix up with deposits and the money coming and going out of different accounts and then back in to them, I'll see to it that they all get their twenty quid back, and you can mind your own business. You get a bit above yourself sometimes, you know, because people kid you on and call you councillor you think it means something, well it disnae, and you can fuck off with all that independence shite as well, who are you to tell everybody that Britain is shite and everything is about tartan and fuckin shortbread tins."

He quietened down and looked me straight in the eye, "My conscience is clear" he said

"That's just a sign of a bad memory" I replied

Peter could see the signs, my voice was getting quieter, that was usually a warning of a volcanic eruption, he had seen them often enough before to recognise the warning signs, he approached the table and took a grip of my elbow and said "Come on Da. I'm starving let's go and join the rest of the boys for a curry, you're wasting your time here, trying to get him to do the right thing is harder than nailing a trifle to a tree"

I smiled at Peter and said "Aye, you're probably right, I think he's a definite no to independence." We both laughed as we walked away, I'm sure Peter never seen the look of loneliness in Pat's eyes as we walked away. I did. I don't think Pat fully appreciated that there was a price to pay for treating people like he did and the bill was overdue.

Surprisingly the night at the curry house was a great laugh, I sat beside Bart Cooper for most of the night and received a lesson in hard drinking, and the rules of life, and a plethora of one liners.

"Do you know what's really enjoyable about being sober Danny?" Bart asked me.

"Naw" I answered.

"Nothing" he said and laughed so hard some of his Guinness came out of his nose.

"But I know I drink too much sometimes, look at last Friday night, I was that drunk I took a bus home, I know that doesn't sound like much, but it was the first time I had ever drove a bus." He added breaking into laughter again.

Bart is a philosophising drinker, no matter how drunk he is he comes out with some gems of wisdom, I asked him "Why do you think Bozo acts so stupid at times" Bart replied "Maybe it's not an act"

He Paused at one point and said "Danny" holding his pint up and admiring the head on it "Drink is never the answer pal, but sometimes it at least makes you forget the question." He seemed to be tickled by my amusement so he kept them coming.

"I phoned up the builder's yard last week and said to the guy on the phone, I want a skip outside my house on Sunday, and do you know what he said Danny"

"Naw" I answered.

"Who's stopping you" he almost rolled off his seat, he laughed so much. I also laughed and just when I had almost stopped he said to me with apparent sincerity "Laughing is good for you Danny, It's like jogging for your insides."

"I had to go down to the RSPCA office last week Danny, it's tiny you couldn'y swing a cat in there" He said again spraying Guinness out of his nose.

The night turned into a joke telling contest until they got more and more stupid as they do. Then as had happened the night before the majority of the drinkers went drinking and clubbing. Later there was a fair bit of anger about Pat, going around but I had no idea it would lead where it did.

Chapter five; Whodunit, in fact who didny do it?

"There's been a murder" Stuart Taggart said to me as I sat down next to him, with my full Scottish the next morning.

I smiled "You really do take your name too seriously at times Stuarty boy, get a fucking life" I said good naturedly.

"No seriously" he said "there has actually been a murder during the night" he said tucking into his own full Scottish.

I asked him "Well call me old fashioned Detective, but should you not be detecting?"

"What the fuck's it got to with me, I'm on a golfing weekend in deepest darkest Ayrshire, let the local plod take care of it, it makes a change for them from chasing sheep shaggers and tottie rustlers" he said mopping up the last of his egg yolk with a bread roll.

"Well there's no use asking your pal Baxter Carter to help, because unless the murder weapon was a steak bake or a Greggs pie, he won't have a Scooby" I suggested.

Just at that a uniformed constable came into the dining room and made an announcement "Ladies and gentlemen, there has been a tragic incident during the night, so unfortunately I have to insist that no one leaves the hotel before we have a chance to speak to them, there are officers at both the front and back doors. After we have spoken to you we will put your names on a list that they will have access to and if you are on that list they will let you leave but only if you are on that list"

He then turned to our table and said "Detective constable Taggart, Detective chief inspector Marshall would like a word if you have a minute please"

At the mention of the name Taggart, Jasper Lemon said in a broad Glaswegian accent "There's been a murder" a couple of people tittered but not many, this sounded serious. But Jasper didn't do serious.

Stuart was probably away for about twenty minutes, when he came back he looked seriously unchuffed, by this time I was sitting with Bart Cooper who had a pint of Guinness in one hand and a cooked breakfast on a roll in the other hand, he said he wanted to try a balanced diet, and held both hands up as if they were a set of scales.

Stuart sat opposite me, beside Bart a few of the other guys had joined us in the dining room and he motioned them over to our table. "Listen guys, you're not going to believe this but that thing during the night, it was Pat McGee" he said and looked up and swept his eyes round all of us.

I exclaimed "Fuck me, who did he kill, was it one of our mob, I knew this was getting out of hand, over twenty quid for fuck sake"

"No Danny, you've got the wrong end of the stick, it's Pat McGee who is dead, and it looks like murder" Stuart said with a shocked expression, I know for a fact, due to conversations I had previously had with Stuart that he is fairly cynical, but I suppose you have to be, to do the extraordinarily difficult job that he does, so it surprised me a little that he seemed shocked.

There was a chorus of for fuck sakes round the table, and Charlie asked "Do they know who done it, Stuart"

Stuart looked all round the room and kept his voice low "Look I canny really tell you'se much about what is happening, cause after all you'se are all technically suspects, because you'se know him and you'se are here with him, although it could be a stranger that killed him I suppose"

"Well he was an easy guy to dislike, you didny need to know him for that long to want to do him in" Peter said. Stuart looked at him with interest and I scowled at him for putting his head above the parapet.

Stuart had another look round the room to make sure he wasn't being overheard and said Billy Paterson and Barney Piper are nowhere to be found have any of you'se seen them this morning"

Nobody answered but everybody glanced at each other, we could all remember big Barney having a go at McGee for the last two nights and where big Barney went wee Billy usually wasn't far away.

"Are you a suspect as well then Stuart?" Peter asked.

"Aye and No" Stuart answered pursing his lips "I've been interviewed, and as I have a watertight alibi, I've been eliminated from the enquiry"

"And I suppose your alibi is that you're a polis and the polis don't do things like that" I said cynically.

"No my alibi is that there was somebody with me all night" Stuart said sheepishly.

"Oh your missus will be pleased you've got such a good alibi" I laughed.

"No, you see that's where it's a bit of a reddy, it was my missus that was with me all night, we're trying for another wean, and it's well last night it was like, the right time sort of thing, her temperature and all that was right and it was the right point in her cycle or something, so she drove down at two in the morning, I gave Baxter his marching orders and bobs your uncle" he said grinning.

"Aye and Stuarts your daddy" I said, a few guys laughed and then looked guilty for doing so considering what was happening.

"So I'm in the clear, and you'se are all in the frame, at the minute DCI Marshall is jumping up and down looking for big oily and wee oily, them two are fucked if they don't have a good reason not to be here" Stuart said, yet again checking for eavesdroppers he continued "There's two of the local plod going through the golf store downstairs looking for clues, apparently the murder weapon was a golf club, and they are looking through all of your golf bags, to see who's missing a club" Stuart whispered.

"What club was it?" Bart Cooper asked.

Charlie and I both sniggered and I said "Does it matter, whatever club he used it did the trick did it not, so the murderer at least got his club selection right if nothing else"

Again a ripple of laughter waved round our circle and Bart said "No, I mean it matters because David Simpson's missing a seven iron, remember he threw it up a tree and by the time he went back for it some toe rag had stolen it, I just meant we could all have a club missing it disnae mean we whacked McGee over the head with it, I've not got a four iron for example"

"I've not got a four iron either" I said "I got a wee rescue wood instead Bart, it's a wee Taylor made twenty two degrees it's a cracker for getting through the rough, you should get yourself one of them mate" Another couple of the guys were talking about what club was missing from their bag and why, and what they had replaced it with.

"For fuck sakes will you listen to yourselves" Stuart said "There's a guy lying dead and you'se are talking about what club your missing, and by the way Bart, nobody whacked him over the head with it, they broke the head off it and stabbed him right through the heart with the shaft, in fact the shaft was just about stuck in the floor beneath the bed, it had went right through him, the heads nowhere to be seen"

I said it but everybody else thought it "Big oily"

Barney Piper, big oily was about six feet two and twenty stone, when he hit his five iron and took a divot, you could fill it with sand and call it a bunker, or fill it with water and call it a water feature, he is a very big and very strong man.

Stuart looked at me and said "I know, that's the first thing I thought, but big Barney's no like that, he wouldn'y hurt a fly"

"I don't know about that" I said " I know he's a great laugh and is up for a bit of fun most of the time, but he was raging about that thing with Jason the other day, he really was, I know I don't know him that well but he was proper raging"

"Raging is one thing Danny, but you would need to be mental to pin somebody to the bed with a five iron" Stuart said.

"Well that makes it worse that's Barney's favourite club" I said trying to be funny but there was a ripple of, what seemed like aye good point, murmurings.

"I'm joking you know, I don't think it was Big Barney, but I know it wisnae me, I'm absolutely shite with a five iron" I said, this did cause laughter in fact Charlie let go of one his big guffaws just as DCI Marshall came into the dining room. What a picture we must have presented to him fourteen or fifteen of us sat around a couple

89

of dining tables laughing our heads off a couple of hours after our friend had been killed by some psycho. I say some psycho but it was starting to sink in that it could have been in fact in all probability it was, one of the Unbearables, I glanced at my compatriots and I must say I wasn't the only one looking round the table with suspicion.

"Gentlemen, can I have your attention please" DCI Mitchell banged a spoon on a dining table directly in front of him to quell the hubbub caused by us laughing and the rest of the room tutting about our laughing, there was a couple of old biddies in particular who looked as if the gates of hell had opened and we had all poured out of it.

"Gentlemen please, and ladies" the DCI nodded at the old biddies "As the constable told you earlier on, there was an incident at approximately four thirty am this morning which has tragically resulted in a loss of life, I do apologise but there is no alternative to having you all remain here for the rest of the day, we will be taking statements from everyone who was resident in the hotel so please be patient, I am sure you understand the gravity of the situation, DC Taggart could you come with me please" Stuart stood up and walked out of the room with the DCI who had a conspiratorial hand on his shoulder as he whispered something to Stuart, whatever he was whispering, Stuart looked perturbed.

"Fuckin arsehole" Charlie exclaimed, which was unlike him, I use swear words like punctuation marks, I can't manage a sentence without one, Charlie however normally needs to be riled before resorting to foul language. I looked at him and raised my eyebrows in a gesture universally known as "What's up with you?"

"I was really looking forward to playing Dundonald today and it looks like that's not going to happen because of Pat McGee, if he wasn't dead, I would kill him myself" He said and walked towards the bar "Anybody want a drink?" he asked.

I checked my watch, ten thirty am, this was going to be a very long day.

I was interviewed at about one o'clock, I was probably nearer the beginning of the queue rather than the end, the young Constable came into the bar and asked if I would mind going to conference room A, where I would be asked to supply a witness statement.

I hadn't actually witnessed anything, but it might have been counter productive to make any smart arse remarks at the moment, maybe later eh?

As I entered conference room A, which was basically a square room which could probably hold thirty to forty people either in the rows of plastic chairs which were stacked along the back wall, or at the six tables which were laid out in a sort of classroom arrangement, with everybody facing a white board which was wall mounted. At one side of the first table you came to, were DCI Marshall and surprisingly Stuart Taggart. I was invited to sit opposite them with my back to the door.

Stuart said "Sit down Danny, Sir this is Danny McCallister, Danny has only recently joined both Happy Valley golf club and the unbearables golf society"

"As you can see Danny, can I call you Danny" The DCI, paused to see me nod my approval, "Well as you can see Danny, I have asked DC Taggart to assist me in taking the statements, this is primarily as a means of speeding up the process DC Taggart," again he paused and smiled at me "Sorry I need to suppress a giggle every time I mention his name, Taggart eh? And still he joined the polis, even though he knew the pish taking he would need to suffer, brave lad"

Stuart looked at me and I looked back at him, it was uncanny that we were both thinking the same thing at the same time "Arsehole" or maybe not that remarkable.

"What can you tell us Danny about where you were at 4.30 am this morning" he asked.

"Not much, I was sleeping" I answered.

"Are you positive" he asked.

"Well that's a bit of an existential question if you don't mind me saying officer, you see I was sleeping and as such I had no idea that I was sleeping because when you are sleeping you can't respond to external stimuli, well you can but only physically not mentally, so to ask if I am sure I was sleeping is an existential impossible to answer question, I think therefore I am conscious, I sleep therefore I'm not conscious, do you know what I mean, if I am actually asleep I don't really know that I am asleep because when I am asleep I am unconscious, so when I say I was sleeping, I meant I was sleeping"

I smiled Stuart smiled and almost sniggered the DCI looked confused and said "Right, so you never heard anything" I went into another monologue about how if I was sleeping and heard anything then that would have meant that whatever I heard must have woke me up and de facto I wouldn't have been sleeping any longer, I think I was starting to annoy him, which was okay because he was starting to annoy me by asking stupid questions.

He shook his head and tried again "Was there anybody with you? who can vouch that you were sleeping"

"Ah" I said "That's where this becomes interesting because Peter my son was in the same room as me so technically you should be able to say that he can vouch for me, but can he really, because as far as I know he was also sleeping, I am basing that on the fact that he came in about three o'clock rat arsed drunk and was sleeping by two minutes past three and was still sleeping when I went downstairs for breakfast at half eight, so in point of fact since I was sleeping I don't actually know if he was sleeping and if he was sleeping he wouldn't actually be able to tell you if I was sleeping, tricky one eh?"

He looked at me and started writing on the pad in front of him mumbling as he wrote "Came in at three o'clock you say"

I sighed "Yes, he came in stood in the toilet having a very long piss probably about a ten pinter, then farted like thunder in a tunnel, I pretended I was asleep because I canny be arsed with drunk people even my son, wanting to tell me a lot of shite at three in the morning, he came out of the toilet stood by the bed to take his shoes off and promptly fell on to the top of the duvet, snoring as soon as his head hit the pillow, I gave him a minute, then took his shoes off, loosened his belt to make him comfortable, got back into my own bed and fell asleep reasonably quickly I think, but I wasn't looking at the clock when I actually fell asleep"

"Did you hear anything or anybody else before you fell asleep, anyone in the corridor perhaps" he asked.

"Do you mean did I hear anybody screaming, I'm going to kill you Pat, or anything that sounded like somebody being stabbed with a golf club, or somebody weeping what have I done whilst walking along the corridor" I asked sarcastically.

"Mr McCallister, you are getting quite close to being charged with obstructing the police in a line of enquiry, now answer me clearly, did you hear anything at all that could be relevant?"

"No I didn't" I answered, even I knew playtime was over.

"For background, Mr McCallister are you aware of any reason for anyone to have a grudge against Mr McGee, or for anybody to harbour ill will against him" He asked, I noticed it was now Mr McCallister and not Danny.

"I'm sure Stuart, DC Taggart has filled you in on the problems over the last couple of days, but I wouldn't think any of that was a good reason for somebody getting topped" I said.

"Mr McCallister, there's never a good reason for murder, in my experience it is almost always a pathetic act carried out by a pathetic character for pathetic reasons, if there is anything at all you think may be relevant, you really must let us know, if you don't wish to put it on record have a quiet word with DC Taggart, I have seconded him on to this enquiry, now unless you have anything else to add, I have many more people to interview" He said looking down at his papers in an act of dismissal.

I felt guilty, "I'm sorry for being an idiot today, listen there is something I heard a while back, but it feels as if I am being a grass if I mention it."

"Spit it out Danny, we don't have time for any more shite come on" Stuart said, even he was pissed off with me.

"There was a rumour a while back that when Walter Hagen's missus was seeing somebody else it might have been Pat, and there was one time when young Shagger, I mean Randy Hagen told me he could do Pat in for what he done to his Ma and Da. In fact, this is quite funny if you have a dark sense of humour, he said to me that he was going to batter him over the head with a five iron" I said feeling even more guilty, Walter and his boy were probably going to get some trouble now, and probably for nothing. But I couldn't not say anything, a man was dead after all.

Just as I came back into the dining room, I saw Barney Piper struggling with the young policeman who had asked me to go to conference room A.

"Let go off my arm, you half wit, I'm not going anywhere" Barney said pulling his arm away. His action in pulling his arm away caused the young cop to stumble and fall to his knees, as he did three other policemen, who had presumably heard the commotion ran into the dining room and were all over Barney within seconds, and they weren't gentle.

This caused a furore amongst all of us with cries of that's enough, and get the fuck off him, there were one or two, noticeably Billy Paterson and Igor Currie who weighed in and tried getting between the polis and big Barney. Stuart Taggart appeared in the doorway and appealed for calm from both the polis and the golfers, well that was his intention I'm sure when he shouted "For fuck sake cut it out will you"

Peace descended, slowly. It was only as everybody settled down I noticed Jamie McArthur and Andy Ingles sitting at a table in the corner of the dining room eating sandwiches whilst having a pint and watching the floor show.

"What happened there" I asked as I sat down opposite Andy.

"Big and wee oily came in through the patio doors and the wee polis there, asked Barney who he was, when Barney gave him his name he started grabbing at his arm and trying to manhandle him, brave wee bastard isn't he" Jamie answered giggling.

Andy whacked him with his rolled up newspaper and said "He wisny asking you stupit he was asking me" he then looked at me and said "What he said"

Billy Paterson came over and joined us "Is that right McGee's dead, for fuck sake, that was a bit of a commotion wasn't it" he said breathlessly, "Who killed him do you know yet, it could be anybody everybody hated the fat fucker"

"That's a bit harsh Billy, I don't think anybody hated him, everybody was pissed off at him but hate's a bit harsh, and it's hardly a reason to fucking do him in is it" I said. "Where have you'se two been anyway?" I added.

"We were coming down to breakfast at about eight o'clock, and Barney wanted to check if he had brought his waterproofs cause it looked a bit cloudy, so we went in to the golf store and he had a look through his bag, and he noticed there was no five iron in his bag, he disnae know if he's left it on the course yesterday or some bastard has nicked it, but who would nick one of Barneys clubs, their almost antique, so we were away down to the pro-shop at Prestwick St Nicholas because they had a good sale on the other day." Billy said looking at our reactions he was obviously wondering what he had said wrong.

Andy said "Whoever killed Pat did it by stabbing him with a five iron"

Billy looked round all of us and said "No fuckin way, Barney widnae do anything like that and you'se all know it, so you'se can cut out that shite, if Barney did that prick in it would have been with a single punch he widnae need a weapon for fuck's sake"

"Good point well made" Jamie said and took another bite of his sandwich.

After about an hour Stuart Taggart appeared in the doorway and motioned me over.

"Let everybody know that Barney might get charged with murder, it's just came back from forensics that his fingerprints are on the five iron used to kill McGee, and I also think it's his club" He whispered.

I answered "It probably is his club, he noticed it was missing this morning, but that disnae mean it was him, if somebody just took a random club and it happened to be his then obviously his prints would be on it."

"Aye ok detective McCallister, we have thought of that, but Walter Hagen who is in the next room to the two oily's told us he heard Barney's room door opening in the middle of the night, he wisnae sure what time but he thought it was just after four" Stuart raised his eyebrows in a gesture of it's not looking good is it. I shook my head in confirmation that indeed it wasn't. "Aye but Walter might have his own reasons for fingering Barney, if you can pardon the expression" I said to Stuart.

I went back to the table, by this time another half dozen of our number had joined us, just as I reached the table Barry Monk was outlining his theory.

"I think it was Jason" he said looking round to make sure Jason wasn't in the room.

"Based on what Barry" Peter asked "that you seen him coming out of the bushes at the left of the hotel or was it the right?"

Barry missed the joke and continued "No son, I never seen him in any bushes, no, I think it was him because of the other day, I've never seen him so angry and I've known him for thirty years or more"

"He ripped his card up and walked out, it's hardly a massive hissy fit Barry" I said grinning.

"It is for him son, and anyway you never seen him later on, he's sharing a room with me, and he was saying to me how devastated he felt, it was as if he was being accused of cheating and do you know what he says, he says to me, twenty years ago I would have put one on his chin for treating me like that and I said, if it was me twenty minutes ago I would have put one on his chin, and he said aye maybe I should have and then he said something I think is the clincher" He paused for dramatic effect.

"It's not the fuckin X factor Barry, get on with it" I said.

He looked round all of us and said "He'll get his someday, that's what he said, He'll get his someday, now what else could that mean son, surely he got up during the night and did him in while he was sleeping"

"What do you mean Barry" Jamie McArthur asked, "Do you mean that Jason was sleepwalking while he did it, is that possible?"

"No while Jason was sleeping, while Pat was sleeping stupit" Said Andy as he struck Jamie again with the rolled up newspaper, I remembered a puppy I had once that I used to house train with a rolled up newspaper, maybe Andy was trying the same thing with Jamie.

"I'm telling you son, I know Jason very well and he was absolutely raging inside, he disnae show much emotion but I can assure you, he was angry enough to do that bastard in, I would have done it for him if he had asked, the only doubt I have was whether he could have got out of our room without me hearing him, I've got the hearing of a ninja, a mouse farting can wake me up. So that's a bit of a spanner in the works, unless he slipped something in my wee cup of cocoa right enough that's possible, and our room is right above Pat's" Barry said.

I am not saying you can dismiss Barry's theory lightly but what a lot of shite, Jason the octogenarian assassin, drugs his senior citizen roommate's cocoa and climbs down a rope made from his bed sheets, into the hotel room below, presumably with Barney's five iron clasped in his teeth, (or his gums, I don't know if Jason's teeth are real or not). Bearing in mind that he would have had to get the five iron before eight o'clock because the golf store was locked up by eight every night. I don't think the polis will be assigning many detectives to this particular theory.

"How are you feeling this morning Barry" I asked him "Do you feel as if you have been drugged at all, any nausea, sickness, diarrhoea or anything"

"Well my stool was a bit soft this morning now you come to mention it" he nodded and looked round the table for back up. None came.

Chapter six; The noose tightens

I went for a walk just to try and clear some of the nonsense people had been talking from my head. DCI Mitchell had authorised everybody to go home, Barney was being held for further questioning, and it looked like the polis thought they had their man.

I was sitting staring out at the sea when Stuart Taggart came along and sat beside me.

"Ok porky one" I asked light heartedly.

"You can fuckin talk" he said nodding at my belly and grinning.

"So what's up, are you here to arrest me" I asked.

"No yet, your porn secret's safe with me" he answered then put a serious face on "How well do you know the Cavalier" he asked.

"Charlie Gilhooley" I said with surprise "Well he sort of works in the same building with me and we play golf together that's about it, if I'm honest I know more about his swing than I do about him"

"Do you know that he did eight years for manslaughter in the early eighties" he said.

"Fuck off, I don't believe you" I said, completely shocked. "Absolutely no way, he goes a bit mental at himself when he hits a duff shot, but I have never seen him get upset at anybody else, it just disnae happen"

"He got into a road rage incident with some ned from Easterhouse, apparently the guy sideswiped overtook him and then reversed back into him, just because Charlie had cut him up at some lights, the thing is Danny and this you will find even harder to believe, he killed the guy with a golf club that he had lying in the back seat of the car." Stuart told me, actually grinning.

"Fuck off, next thing you will be saying is, that it was a five iron" I said laughing at the absurdity of the coincidence.

Stuart just nodded and almost dissolved into tears of laughter.

"For fuck sake, what's the chances of that" I asked "That surely canny be a coincidence, fuck me is the wee laughing cavalier a serial killer, that's just so fuckin weird, is it no?" I was stunned I didn't know what to think. This was actually a bit scary, I thought I was a half decent judge of character, but fuck me, this was bizarre, I would have bet my life that Charlie wouldn't be capable of this.

Actually perhaps I had, when I think of all the times I wound him up out on the course when it was just the two of us, he could have turned on me at any time, my knees actually trembled slightly, it's fortunate I was sitting down.

"So what now" I asked, my head still spinning "Will you pick him up, I think he pissed off about an hour ago"

"We have" Stuart replied "We caught up with him on the M77 on his way home, he's being taken to the Kirkintilloch nick for further questioning, we want you and Peter to come in and give statements about his general bad temper" Stuart said tentatively.

"Don't start trying to fit him up Stuart, I never said he had a bad temper, I said he lost the rag with his self sometimes and occasionally threw his clubs about or smashed one against his bag but.." I hesitated realising just what I was saying, and seeing him nod and put a think about it look on his face "No, no, you're taking that the wrong way, that's just golf we all have a wee tantrum from time to time, come on look at Barry Monk for fuck sake, he looks like he's doing a strong man act at times the way he bends his clubs over his head. We all lose the nut with the stupid game, that disnae mean we could do somebody in"

"But he has Danny, that's the big difference, he has" Stuart said with some regret in his voice, "Anyway, we need an official statement from you and your boy, do you want to do it here or come in to Kirky nick tomorrow, it's your shout"

In the end we gave statements there and then it only took an hour and both of us said much the same thing, Charlie was one of the good guys, a bit harsh on himself at times but otherwise wouldn't say boo to a goose, I felt confident that whatever had happened when he was younger, he must have been provoked beyond endurance, I mean he would only have been a teenager at the time so it was well out of order bringing that up now, who the fuck didn't do things they now regret when they were a teenager. Although I do concede stoving somebody's head in with a five iron is a bit worse than smoking hash and being sick in your grannies knicker drawer.

Charlie didn't come in to the office for a few days and when he did he looked a bit gaunt, in fact he looked as if he hadn't slept for the three days we had been back.

He walked into my office and hovered by the door, as he usually does when he has anything to say.

"What have you heard" he asked me.

"Come all the way into the office, so as I can see whether you have a five iron in your hand" I said smiling,

To his eternal credit he guffawed his usual guffaw. "I've heard that the polis want to dig up something from when you were a wee laddie, and use it against you now, and I know that I think they should go fuck themselves, apart from that I've heard fuck all" I said.

Unusually for him he came in and sat down "The bastards are turning me upside down and inside out, they have searched my house, searched all the computers at home and in here, as you well know" he said exasperated.

"Have they found your stash of gay porn" I asked

"You know that's not my gay porn that belongs to Bryan Hinter downstairs" he smiled, actually we both smiled Bryan did have an impressive stash of gay porn, impressive if you are into that sort of thing I mean.

"Joking aside Danny, they are really doing a number on me, my sons are worried about it getting into the papers, they don't actually know what happened back in 1982, my wife and I can't decide whether to tell them or not, it's a monumental fuck up, and all because somebody took it into their head to put Pat McGee out of his misery" He paused and looked me in the eye.

"It wasn't me" he said.

"I know" I said looking him straight in the eye.

"So who was it then" he asked "Any ideas, because the sooner they catch the dickhead, the sooner I get my life back"

"I don't know" I answered "It's got to be one of our mob though hasn't it, I mean what's the odds of it being a stranger."

"Aye , you're right it must be, who though, who would actually be capable of stabbing him to death with a broken golf club, I still canny believe it, when you actually say it out loud it sounds ludicrous, one of the Unbearables has actually done this, it's surreal" Charlie said forlornly.

"It's not that surreal Charlie, who would have believed that you could kill somebody, certainly not me" I said, a silence descended for about a minute before I carried on.

"Let's make a list then, let's pool what we know and what we've heard and make a list of who it could have been, I'll start, you, naw, what about me?" I hesitated to smile at him and he said "No" and smiled back.

"Peter, No, and that's the only three I am absolutely sure would be a naw" I said.

"Hold on Danny, surely you don't think any of the old boys could have done it, Jack, Jason, Barry Monk, Rob the Geordie, Harry Caravan, surely we can rule all of them out straight away, most of them would have struggled to get up to his room without using the lift" Charlie suggested.

"Don't kid yourself most of them are fitter than you and me, but I agree none of them are likely to have done it but then who is?" I said.

"Barney Piper, Billy Paterson, David Simpson and Igor Currie, them four for a start. You know how tight they are it could be any one of them and they would all cover up for each other, look how protective they are just about their kitty, they would do anything to get a fiver in it" Charlie suggested.

"Right ok, you've said four so I'll give you another four, Walter Hagen and young Shagger, Jasper lemon and Bart Cooper" I offered. "Walter and shagger because of the rumours about Walters's wife

104

and Pat McGee, even Walter isnae sure if that was true or not, Jasper Lemon because he is stupid enough to do anything and he was pissed and shouting his mouth off about Pat, a couple of hours before the dastardly deed was done" I offered.

"Okay so far but why Bart Cooper, I wouldn't think him capable" Charlie said.

"Well I don't know Charlie, Bart's a very moral guy, he's got a very serious sense of right and wrong, I'm not saying he's like superman out there fighting against evil, but he was really angry about Pat disrespecting old Jason the way he did, he was also very drunk and I think he could easily have got into a fight with Pat" I argued.

"Okay I get your point Danny but, this wisnae a fight, if somebody had stood up in a pub and thumped Pat I would agree that it could well be Bart that done it, but this somebody waited until Pat was sleeping, sneaked in and stabbed him with the shaft of a golf club" Charlie said.

"How do you know he sneaked in and stabbed him, whoever did it could have been sitting talking to him and then done it, for all we know pat invited them into the room" I said, speculating.

"At half past four, I doubt it" Charlie said.

"Why do you doubt it, it's possible, think about it. Pat gets woke up by somebody making a noise in the corridor, pops his head to have a moan see that it's an Unbearable, talks or argues for a minute or two and says, come in out of the corridor before we wake the whole hotel up" I said.

"Maybe, except for a couple of things, this random guy in the corridor would first of all have to have nicked big Barney's five iron and then when he was in Pat's room wait for him to fall asleep and then kill him, because the police told me that Pat was sleeping when he was stabbed they made a big deal of it actually, trying to make me feel guilty for doing him in whilst he slept and had no chance to defend himself" Charlie said.

 Then he looked pensively at me as if unsure whether he should actually say what he said next "And while I think about it Danny, the ned that I killed way back then, screamed at me that he was going to stab my fuckin cunt in, that's exactly what he said, what a strange thing to say, I panicked and whacked him once with the golf club as he ran at me, it turned out it wasn't a knife in his hand it was a bunch of keys"

"None of my business Charlie or anybody else's to be honest, but my suspicions about Bart still stand it could have been him just because I can imagine him standing up for somebody like Jason" I said.

"Fair enough but that's at least eight people already we need to whittle them down more than that, I'll tell you what by the end of the week let's try to have three names each, and we will see if any agree and maybe try to dig up some more info by talking to everybody that was there" he said.

"So who does that make us, Cagney and Lacey or Bodie and Doyle or Scooby doo and Shaggy" I suggested, Charlie guffawed and said "Randall and Hopkirk and you'll be Hopkirk if you're not careful"

A death threat from a convicted killer, happy days.

I did indeed give it a lot of thought over the course of that week and settled on four likely candidates I just couldn't get it down to three, Charlie did get it down to three, the only one he missed out was Jasper Lemon, I had a strange feeling that Jasper knew something or was hiding something the day of the murder, he wasn't his usual self, I suppose you could think that a murder in the vicinity would subdue anybody, that doesn't apply to Jasper, I think normally he would have been drawing chalk outlines of murder victims in each corridor of the hotel, or he at least would shave his head and take up sucking lollipops. The fact that he wasn't larking about that day, in fact from what I can remember he was nowhere to be seen for most of the day, that is suspicious in my eyes, there was an opportunity to be the centre of attention and he never took it, very strange.

The three we agreed on where Barney Piper, as much as we both liked the big man, he was very pissed off at Pat McGee and verbal about it the night Pat died, and he was one of the few with the strength to drive a golf club shaft right through someone's body.

We also agreed on Billy Paterson as a potential suspect, Billy was one of the most vocal critics of Pat McGee and what he had been accused of, my one doubt was that he doesn't give the impression that he would be prepared to get physical, he did give Pat McGee a piece of his tongue on more than one occasion, Charlie's opinion is that he was capable of this act, I wasn't so sure but left him on the list just because of his verbal attacks on McGee.

Igor Currie was the third suspect we agreed on, Igor had the size and strength to carry out the murder in the manner that it was, and he was also vocally critical of McGee in a massive way, in fact more so than anyone else,, he was prepared to call it as he saw it and outright accuse McGee of being a thief.

My money was on Igor, Charlie favoured big Barney Piper. Peter incidentally thought that it was possible that Barry Monk had bent a five iron over his head whilst arguing with McGee, which subsequently broke accidentally piercing McGee's heart, so really the whole thing could have been an accident. Bollocks.

"So what's our plan of action, our strategy, how do we get to the bottom of this" Charlie asked me, as we sat in his office with a coffee on the Friday afternoon following our return from the golf outing.

"Well, this Sunday we need to try and make sure we are out with one or more of the suspects each, so we can quiz them" I suggested.

"What? Do you really think anybody will be playing this week after what happened" Charlie asked with surprise written all over his face.

I answered equally surprised "Do you think there won't be, it's the unbearables, it's a Sunday morning, we play golf that's what we do. If Pat McGee's funeral was Sunday morning there's a fifty fifty chance that we might pause between shots as his hearse drove by, but it would only be fifty fifty. Are you no going on Sunday?"

"Well, I wasn't sure but I may as well if you think everybody else will be" Charlie said still unconvinced that there would be a full turn out on Sunday.

There was. The smoker's room was packed, Igor Currie did the decent thing and stood up and made a speech regarding the circumstances of Pat's death.

"Order, order" he shouted as he banged his hand on the table he was sat behind, trying to quell the babble of conversations going on around the room.

"As you all know, Pat's dead, me and Billy Paterson will take over the organising and Peter McCallister will put up all the scores on the unbearables website" He then sat down, I for one, was very touched by his moving rendition of his heartfelt speech regarding the demise of Pat McGee.

I fiddled the draw with Peter's help so that I was out with both Jasper lemon and Billy Paterson, Jason McKechnie made up the fourball. I was paired with Jasper. It was a nice bright spring morning and we should have all been looking forward to having a pleasant round of golf, if there is such a thing, but as blasé as we all liked to imagine ourselves, the death of Pat McGee was having an effect on us all.

"So who do you think killed the cheating thieving fat bastard, Danny" Billy Paterson asked me as we strolled down the path to the first.

"Wow, say what you mean Billy why don't you" I laughed

"Well I'm not going to be a hypocrite, I didnae like him and I thought he was a thieving fat bastard, so I say it like I see it" He said adamantly.

"I know, Billy, but getting done in is a bit severe is it no, would it not be enough just to throw him out of the unbearables, is killing him not just a bit harsh" I asked him.

"You seem to be sticking up for him, is it alright with you that he stole from us, we were his mates" Billy asked me, I felt as if I was being accused of being in collusion with McGee because I wasn't prepared to condemn him out of hand.

"Billy, he wasn't my mate, he was somebody I play golf with on a Sunday and personally I don't give a rat's scrotum if he had his fingers in the petty cash tin, which by the way was never proved. I just don't think that anybody deserves to be put to death for having a wee fiddle going on the side, do you?" I said bluntly.

"No, don't get me wrong what happened was terrible, a tragedy. But nobody even knows if it was to do with him being a cheat and a thief, it could have been something else for all we know, maybe he was shagging somebody's wife again, or robbing somebody else who knows, whatever, he's dead so it disnae really matter now does it, whoever did it, did it, if the polis catch them fine and if they don't they don't. It's nothing to me either way." Billy said pretending indifference.

"But Billy, let's just say one of the unbearables killed him because of the twenty quid, he nicked from everybody, what if you draw this guy in a round of the singles and he thinks, you cheated, let's say you took a drop when you shouldn'y have, do you think he will come and kill you as well, because after all, it's worth more than twenty quid to win the singles" I asked.

"I don't cheat" Billy replied affronted by the suggestion that he did.

"That's not the point, I know you don't cheat but what if he thought you did, or what if I cheated and he caught me, do you think he would kill me as well. It's important this guy gets caught Billy because if he can do it once he will do it again, and it could be you or me next, even though you don't cheat and I try not to" I said ominously.

"He wouldn'y do that it's only because it was McGee that he got done in" Billy said in response.

"Do you know who done this Billy, because how do you know he wouldn't do it again and that it was only because it was McGee, or it wouldn't have happened, was it you?" I said hurriedly hoping to catch him off guard. As if he would admit it to me under any circumstances

"Don't talk pish" He said, selecting a club from the bag.

"Is that your total defence, "Don't talk pish", no alibi or anything just "Don't talk pish", I hope the jury buy it for your sake" I said selecting a club from my bag.

"I thought he was an arsehole, but I didnae kill him, I don't particularly care who did either, if that makes me a bad person, sue me" he said, and took his tee shot swiping it down the middle.

"Good shot" I said, "what did you hit there?"

"My five iron" he answered grinning "It's my favourite club now"

I worked on Jasper Lemon next, although he was very difficult to engage with that day, he was very morose and introverted not like himself at all.

We were both in the right hand rough on the sixth hole, and we were being held up by the fourball in front which included Harry Caravan, naturally. "So who done it Jasper" I asked him, he was standing by his bag looking down at his ball. He seemed lost in his own thoughts it was actually a shame to disturb him, Jasper doesn't often stop and think, in fact he doesn't often think at all.

His head jerked up as if he had been punched "Who did what?" he asked spinning round to see if he had missed something happening.

"Who did the dirty deed on Pat McGee, oh here, that could be a country western song couldn't it" I said to him and started singing

"Pat was fat, Pat was a cheat poor old Pat now feels no heat" in a western drawl.

"Why should I give a fuck?" he asked me belligerently.

"You don't need to give a fuck it was only a wee song ya fanny, and don't snarl at me" I said taking umbrage at his tone.

"No, why should I give a fuck who done him in, que sera sera." He said, obviously, in my opinion, trying to close the conversation down.

"What the fuck's up with you" I asked "Who stabbed a hole in your condom" I said laughing.

He looked round and said "I think the polis will be coming to lift me anytime" He was looking genuinely worried. "I've done something stupit, I canny fuckin believe how stupit, I don't know why I canny believe it, because I am always doing something fuckin stupit but this is really serious, oh for fuck sake I am a fanny at times, I really am."

I thought about it for a few seconds, did I really want to get involved here, this wisnae the laugh I thought it might be, and Jasper was genuinely scared. But then again that didn't mean it wouldn't be a laugh to get him mortally terrified if I could.

"Did you kill him like" I asked all innocently.

"Naw, don't be a fanny, of course I didnae, I don't care enough about him to kill him, he was an eejit" Jasper said, again looking around shiftily. "But my DNA is all over his hotel room and I canny believe they haven't came looking for me, I've hardly slept all fuckin week, I'm a nervous wreck and she is biting the head off me because all I do is toss and turn all through the night, every night since we came hame"

I laughed out loud "How the fuck did your DNA get in his hotel room, where you and him having an affair, were you having a ham shank while he watched, spill the beans, ya fanny"

"The night before he got kebabbed, I went into his room with a bottle of pish and threw it all over his sheets and some of it went on his carpet. I thought it would be funny when the maid came in to change his bed if it was covered in pish. But now after what's happened my pish is all over his hotel room, what the fuck are the polis going to think." He said grinning.

"They are going to think the same as me, that you stabbed him to death in a perverted sex ritual that included you marking the territory round his bed by pishing on it. You're fucked, that's life, the greens clear is it you or me to go" I said and walked back to my bag to select a club for my next shot. I turned to him and did give a piece of advice, "I think you better go and find Stuart Taggart, and tell him about your stupidity, to be fair he already Knows how stupit you are but, you better tell him exactly what you did, it's better you telling him than him coming to find you"

Jason was on good form that day, both in his golf game where he was hitting the sweet spot regular and in his demeanour.

"You're in a good mood this morning Jason" I said as we walked off the eighth tee.

"Aye, well why not it's a nice day and I'm playing well" He said.

"Different from last week then, what a nightmare that was eh, a bit out of order getting stabbed over a game of golf isn't it" I said.

113

His mood darkened, never let it be said that I can't bring somebody down when they are too happy, I'm an expert.

"That wisnae about golf son, there's definitely more to it than that" he said walking slightly quicker down the hill, as if he wanted to distance himself from the subject, I couldn't let that happen could I.

"So what do you mean more to it, have you heard something like?" I asked, out of breath trying to catch up with him, these old buggers can move when they want to, or maybe I'm too fat, no these old buggers are like hares at times that's what it is.

"Everybody was talking about it on Wednesday morning, Rob Chandler and Jack Sharp have both heard different rumours about McGee, Jack was saying that he heard McGee was sleeping with his bosses wife and Rob heard that he had his fingers in the till at work as well as here, it's a terrible thing all this, I almost never turned up this morning. I got the feeling that some of the people here think that it was my fault some loony killed Pat. I wasn't even that bothered about the scorecard nonsense. But there's no way on earth that somebody killed him because of that, that would be insane." He said and walked away to play his shot, he duffed it. Well done Danny.

Not that it matters but Jason and I won three and two, another pound saved.

I caught up with Charlie in the clubhouse he had been out with Walter and Randy Hagen as well as Andy Ingles.

"Any joy?" I asked him.

"Yes we won two up and I had a sixty six" he answered.

"Not the golf ya fanny, any info on the murder I mean" I said.

114

"No, not much, I didn't really like to bring it up" he said taking a sip from his orange juice and soda water.

"What does that mean you didnae like to bring it up, you would rather the polis pin it on you then, rather than you being thought of as socially indelicate, you have a strange way of looking at things sometimes, so you never found out anything or asked anything, nothing at all?" I asked exasperated.

"Well, Andy reckoned it was definitely McGee that was seeing Walter's wife when they split up, and he also said that when Randy heard about it, him and McGee had a right barney about it in the locker room, young Randy was threatening to rip his head off apparently, but this was all two years ago or longer than that even, it's old news really" Charlie told me.

"Not necessarily, things like that can fester, maybe the bold shagger has just been biding his time and waiting for his chance to do some damage, you never know, he's a big strong boy, he could have done it." I said looking over at Randy, who was having a laugh with his old man and Peter.

"Well that's no great is it, that just adds somebody else to the list it doesn't take anybody off it" Charlie said shaking his head.

"I think we can cross off Jasper and Billy Paterson, I had a good talk with both of them and I don't think they were involved, Jasper did something really Jasper like but he didnae kill him and Billy isn't capable he's angry and mouthy but I don't think he would actually go that far" I said, taking a closer look at Randy Hagen, he seemed to be laughing a bit too much, he looked over full with nervous energy, I think a wee chat was in order.

I waited until Peter got up to go to the bar and I nicked his seat beside Randy. "How you doing bold boy, play well today then did you?" I asked Randy as I sat beside him patting him on the back as I did so.

"Naw, Shite" he said.

"Naw, shite is that it no saying what score you had or what went wrong or the bits that were maybe ok" I asked.

"Naw, I was shite" he said.

"Your quite a raconteur, quite a conversationalist when you get going you, aren't you" I said

"What?" he said.

Rather than trying to ease my way gently into a conversation and gently prise information from Randy I tried a different tactic.

"Who do you think killed Pat McGee, it wisnae you was it" I asked abruptly.

His eyes darkened, I've noticed that before about Randy, even when he's all smiles and acting best mates with everybody, there's a darkness behind his eyes, this boy is capable of anything was my immediate thought and I shivered inside a little.

"Why would you ask that Danny, are you trying to accuse me or something" He barked quite abruptly.

"Calm down wee man, I wisnae accusing you of anything, I was just winding you up, it's a wee laugh that's all" I said, I could see he was upset about something just by his body language he had been sitting with legs wide open and taking long swallows from his pint of lager. Now his legs were tight together his left hand was clenched in a fist on his knee and his right hand had a tight grip on his glass, which he was now taking quick sips from and his eyes were blazing, he was coiled tight and angry.

I hesitated for a second or two not sure whether to push him, I didn't want this getting out of hand, but then again in for a penny.

"If I was a polis I would be thinking you had something to hide Shagger, you're getting awfully upset son" I teased.

"I'm not fucking upset at all" he said angrily and apparently squeezed his pint glass too hard because it broke, spilling lager all over the table and down on to his trousers.

He jumped up to avoid the spill as best he could, he still held the remains of the glass in his right hand. He looked down at the jagged bottom half of a pint tumbler and then looked up at me. I am sure I was mistaken, but for the briefest moment I think he imagined what damage that jagged glass in his hand would do to my face, as I said I was probably wrong, sometimes I have a vivid imagination, too vivid.

Chapter seven. Tragedy strikes

My brief encounter with Randy Hagen ended amicably enough. the dark light behind his eyes had gone out and he was all cheery and smiley and flicking the dregs of the lager on the table at Jasper Lemon who had his mouth open trying to catch them, but Randy did glance at me with a look that I interpreted as a warning to keep my nose out, I heard his warning loud and clear, but I do like a challenge.

A couple of days later I bumped into Stuart Taggart, he was just coming off the golf course as I was walking towards the practice area, I occasionally have a flash of inspiration that practicing will help my golf game improve, but normally I have a cold shower and the feeling passes.

"Hi Stuart, how you doing, never seen you on Sunday" I said cheerily.

"Are you fuckin Joking Danny, I shouldn't even be here today but I had a team match to play, I'm going to get changed come in and have a pint with me I'll no be five minutes" He said nodding towards the smoker's room.

I was torn, should I go in and have a pint on a sunny afternoon or should I go and slog up and down that stupid hill in the practice area, alternatively shanking and duffing chip shots as I went. "Okay" I said see you in there.

The bar was virtually empty, two old boys that I had never seen before and three of the juniors who I did recognise, one in particular I had played a few holes with previously, the boy hit a golf ball further than I went on holiday, his swing was poetry in motion, I am sure he will go far.

I got the drinks in, Tennant's lager for Stuart, shandy for me.

"So what's up caught the murderer yet" I asked him as soon as he sat down.

"Give us a break Danny, I'm pig sick of this shit" he hesitated seeing my amusement at the phrase pig sick, "Aye alright excuse the pun, but really this had fuck all to do with me, I was down in Ayrshire happily playing shite golf and all of a sudden I'm up to my knees in this shite because one of you mad bastards decides to do Pat McGee in, my DCI is having fuckin kitten's I'm telling you"

"Oh Dear" I said "How very naughty of Pat to get himself stabbed through the heart with a golf club and spoil your weekend, the bastard"

"You're fuckin spot on the fat ignorant bastard's put me right in the shite" Stuart said.

"Why, you didnae do him in did you?" I asked

"Your interrogation technique is crap Danny, you need to lure the suspect in not just come out with it like that, and anyway I had an alibi remember" he smiled.

"Och aye, you were servicing the missus weren't you, any luck yet with impregnating her, if you're having to do a lot of overtime just now, I'll have a go if you want, I've got two boys, only had sex twice, a 100% success rate, just say the word" I offered.

He quite rightly ignored me and said "My DCI wants me to quit the golf club, he said I canny be seen to be associating with potential murderers"

"Fuck him" I said, as advice goes I think I was straight to the point and the advice itself was sound.

"Aye well, it's not that easy, anyway he's agreed that I shouldn't chuck it yet but try to dig about a wee bit and see what I can find out first" He said.

"Oh, I see, so this is why we are having a pint, so as you can ,what did you say again, lure me in" I said still smiling.

"Well, aye, I suppose so" he said.

"Fair enough, there has been a bit of talk I'll tell you what I've heard." I said and filled him in about my conversations with Billy Paterson and Jasper Lemon.

"We knew about Jasper, he came into the station yesterday, we actually knew that somebody had pished all over the carpet at the bed but since Jasper's DNA isn't on file we had no way to know it was him, he's put himself in the frame and one of the boys is digging about looking at him just now, but it's a wild goose chase, it wisnae Jasper, you should have seen him, he was greeting and everything when he was telling the DCI about throwing the pish, I don't know about pish but he was certainly shitting himself" he laughed and finished his pint.

"Do you want another" he asked, I settled for a soft drink, I had the car, and drinking isn't my favourite sport anyway.

As he settled back into his seat I related my confrontation with Randy Hagen, he waited patiently until I had finished, I could see this had piqued his interest, He sat up much straighter and pushed his second pint to the side, it seemed as if a switch had been turned on and Stuart was now a policeman and not a friend.

"You need to come down the nick and make a statement about that Danny, sorry I can't just ignore it" he said going into full CID mode.

"Okay, I had intended giving you a call and doing that anyway, I Just had to think it through first" I said, being equally serious, this wasn't a joke anymore.

"Why, are you doing this Danny, that's Billy, Jasper and now young Shagger, why are you basically grassing them up to me, what's in this for you" He asked, being a detective I suppose, he likes to ask awkward questions.

"Charlie's a mate and I don't want your mates fitting up my mate if he didn't do anything wrong" I said.

Stuart looked at me pensively, sucked his teeth and thought for a moment "Fair do's" he says, "I'll tell you a couple of things that you never heard from me ok" he looked at me and I nodded my agreement.

"Charlie is in the frame for this, but not completely, there's no physical evidence yet but as far as we can see in the last forty years in Scotland two people have been killed with a golf club, both times it was a five iron and both times Charlie Gilhooley was there, it's too much of a coincidence to ignore" He said.

"Why is the fact that it's a five iron significant, do you actually think Charlie decided to select his club to kill Pat, he stood over Barney's bag and thought, I know I'll use the five iron it did the job perfect the last time. At least I will have confidence in the shot" I said shaking my head. "It is a coincidence and you know it, Charlie told me about what happened when he was young, and I reckon I would have done exactly what he did and to be fair I think anybody would have, including you"

121

"You're not wrong Danny, It should probably have been seen as self defence and if he had only hit the boy once it would have been, but he hit him eight times" Stuart said no longer smiling.

"But how many of them were practice swings" I said, outwardly grinning but inwardly thinking Charlie had left that little detail out, I wonder why.

"What's the script with big Barney, have you'se let him out yet" I asked, I had no wish to dwell on Charlie's deception I would deal with that later.

"Aye, we let him go a couple of days later, but he's still prime suspect, he's got to be, prints all over the murder weapon and no alibi, other than he was full of the booze and out for the count, but since Billy Paterson was well pissed as well there's no way of verifying that, we also have a statement telling us that somebody heard movement in his room at about four o'clock in the morning, it's not exactly a smoking gun, but it's probably enough to charge him. The only reason we're holding off is that the DCI thinks the procurator fiscal would say not enough evidence and shelve it, so we want a bit more before we cuff him. Have you heard anything about him?" he asked expectantly.

"Not a Dickie bird" I said "I would be absolutely completely stunned if it was him, there is no way I think he would do that, I can see him losing his temper in a rumble and thumping somebody with one of his big ham hough fists, but sneaking about in the middle of the night, no chance, I would abandon all faith in my judgement of people if it turned out to be him" I said.

"So you thought that Charlie could do what he did then" Stuart said challenging my assertions about Barney.

"But that proves my point, when you sit back and think about it what Charlie done, anybody could have, you me Barney, anybody. But what was done to McGee was in a different league, this wisnae spur of the moment or self defence, some fucker planned this and then done it, and big Barney's not got that in him, I'd bet my mortgage on it" I said.

"So who has" Stuart asked.

"You're the fuckin detective, you tell me" I said.

I went that evening and officially gave Stuart a statement about young Shagger I didn't particularly enjoy it, I felt guilty, but the image of him glancing at the broken glass and then me with that darkness in his eyes, made me think I was doing the right thing.

The following Sunday it was almost a full house, the only person missing was Stuart Taggart, who was obviously still keeping his distance, well he wasn't the only Unbearable not there, McGee wasn't there either.

The atmosphere was more or less returning to normal, it never ceases to amaze me the way golfers take tragedy in their stride, well to be fair I suppose it's just people and not specific to golfers. But because Golf clubs in general have a very high average age, most golf club members are over fifty and a high percentage are in their seventies and eighties, one of the side effects of this is that through the winter, almost without exception, every week see the lowering of the flag to half mast and a little framed announcement of a members death would be on a table in the hallway as you entered the club house through the members entrance.

This small framed sheet of paper advising members of someone's passing was treated with respect and dignity at all times, there were very few people who didn't glance at it and reflect on their own good fortune. That morning the photograph frame was on the table but it had been turned face down, I lifted it and seen the announcement of the death of pat McGee, I had a flash of anger. Who would be so callous, so undignified to turn this face down, outrageous in my opinion. I walked into the smoker's room fully intending to tell them what I thought of the person who would stoop so low, but before I could I got caught up in a mini row.

"Don't be stupit ya fanny" Andy Ingles was saying to Jamie McArthur, since this was the way Andy reacted to ninety nine per cent of anything Jamie said, it was not unusual in itself, it was Jamie's reply that grabbed my attention.

"It's no stupit, I'm telling you, my cousins boy's girlfriend is a polis and she said that's the rumour doing the rounds about McGee" Jamie said, primarily to Andy, but the whole room had hushed to listen to his wisdom, apparently.

"What did I miss" I asked Jamie, it was Igor that answered me.

"You missed one of McArthur's gems, his nieces uncles aunties best pals next door neighbour has it on good authority that the polis are putting what happened to McGee down to suicide" The room basically exploded with laughter, I must admit I found it hard not to join in.

"I'm just telling you what she told me, I'm not saying it's true" Jamie said defensively.

I said to him "Jamie, according to Stuart Taggart, McGee was lying on his back and the golf club was driven through his heart and through the mattress beneath him, for him to have done that to himself would be impossible, unless his arms were six feet long"

124

Jamie answered "Maybe it was a suicide pack"

Another round of laughter, "Do you mean a suicide pact Jamie and if it was where's the other dead body, a suicide pact means two or more people being involved" I asked.

Jamie answered "Maybe they shit themselves and bolted"

More laughter, "Aye Jamie maybe they did or in fact just stood there at the side of the bed and pished themselves with fear and then bolted" I said and winked at Jasper, his face was a picture, his famous sense of humour seemed to have abandoned him.

Randy Hagen asked me a question above the general hum of conversation and laughter, "When where you talking to Stuart Taggart, Danny"

I looked towards where he was sitting at the window beside his old man and Charlie Gilhooley, he asked again "You said Stuart told you this and Stuart told you that, when was this Danny, are you thinking of joining the polis now, are you not too wee and fat and old for that," It was said in jest I'm sure but I picked up an undercurrent of venom in the question, whether anyone else did or not, I'm unsure although both Barney and Charlie glanced at me neither of them were joining in the laughter.

As luck would have it I was drawn out to play in a fourball with Charlie, Barney and Randy Hagen, although just as that draw was made Randy remembered he had to leave early today and swapped with someone in the first game out, that someone being Lesley Clifford.

It was at the fifth hole that morning that tragedy struck as per the title of this chapter. Some things in life can be taken on board and dealt with, no matter how tragic. Nine eleven, the holocaust, the killing fields. But this was different this was deeply personal. My driver broke, my Taylor made R7, the head came away from the shaft, and it was beyond repair. I wanted to fall to my knees and weep, but refused to show the depth of my despair to my playing partners. My younger brother who is a real golfer with a handicap of five had given me this driver four years ago. Previous to this driver, every other one I tried no matter the make or model, I sliced wildly, before wee David gave me this R7, I played for three years without a driver in my bag at all, reluctantly accepting that I couldn't use a driver.

This R7 had changed this and my handicap dropped by five strokes in three years, the death of Pat McGee was unfortunate but the real tragedy in this whole story is the death of my R7 driver. RIP. I actually managed a half decent round finishing with a sixty eight using my three wood so maybe I exaggerated the effect of my broken driver, a wee bit.

During the round, despite being in mourning for my lamented driver I did pick up an antipathy towards me emanating from Barney and surprisingly Charlie.

"Have you been talking to Stuart Taggart" Barney asked me in the straightforward no nonsense way that Barney approaches everything, call a spade a fuckin shovel and be done with it, is the big man's admirable attitude.

"Aye" I said, "I was up practicing during the week, or rather intending to practice when I bumped into him and he asked if I wanted a pint" I answered, again honestly and straightforward as he deserved.

"You don't drink" he said quite aggressively.

"Thanks for reminding me big man, I forgot that I don't drink" I said sarcastically "I had a shandy and then an orange juice, do you believe me now, that I just randomly bumped into him, or do you think I'm a super grass on the take from Taggart, the hardened chain smoking detective"

"Stuart disnae smoke" he said and grinned.

I relaxed "Straight up big man I did bump into him, we had a shandy and a gab, he said nothing about the case, his balls would be on the chopping board if he talked about that to any of us, that's why he's not coming down on Sundays and just sneaking in midweek, he canny associate with riff raff like us, especially if one of us done McGee in, did you?" I asked semi seriously.

"Naw, mores the pity" he said "It couldn'y be any worse even if I had, the polis are all over me, it's ludicrous. They have been taking fingerprints, DNA samples, going through all the computers in the house even the grandwean's wee ipad, it's bloody awful, the wife's up to high doh. Even this morning she was shouting at me for coming up here, it will only bring more trouble she shouted at me as I left the house. It's really getting on my nerves, just because somebody did the thieving bastard in, I'm getting all this hassle"

"Charlie said exactly the same when they questioned him" I said and immediately regretted it.

"Why did they question him" Barney was on it like a shot.

"Oh I don't know, I think it was while we were all at the hotel, he was just saying what a pain in the arse it all was with all the questions and that" I tried to extricate myself from the shite I had dropped myself in.

127

He looked at me with great suspicion but said nothing, he did have a look over at Charlie though, with a look that suggested he might pursue this a bit further given the chance. Then a few holes later I was walking down a fairway with Charlie and he started quizzing me, but I had just about had enough, I was being piggy in the middle here and none of it was my problem, well except of course that I had been sticking my nose in since day one, but I didn't consider that at the time.

"You never mentioned that you were talking to Stuart during the week" Charlie said with an air of suspicion in his question.

"You never mentioned that you beat that young boy over the head eight times either" I replied with anger and stared straight at him.

He paled visibly and said "I'd appreciate it if you could manage to keep your voice down" he said nervously checking to see if we could have been overheard.

"And I would have appreciated it, if you had told me the truth, and no made it seem you were an innocent victim, you hit him on the head with a golf club eight times for fuck sake" I said in a loud whisper.

He responded to me also in a loud whisper, anybody looking on would have been able to compare it to scenes in supermarkets we have all seen before, of a married couple having a row in a supermarket both of them whisper shouting at each other and completely unaware that everybody knows what they are doing. Except Charlie and I had a trolley each.

"I didn't tell you the details because you didn't need to know, I told you what happened the fact that I panicked and kept hitting him because I was shit scared had actually fuck all to do with you" he said red faced.

I wasn't happy but he had a fair point, "Alright" I said "No need to lose your temper about it, and start swinging a golf club about" I said it with a smile, if I hadn't, judging by the look on his face I might have ben spending the next couple of days trying to have a five iron removed from my arse.

I did see him and Barney deep in conversation beside Charlie's car after the game. When I asked Charlie later he told me that he had filled Barney in on the whole situation as they were both more or less in the same boat, suspects in a murder that neither had committed, according to them anyway.

The next couple of weeks passed incident free, well not completely incident free there was the usual squabbling about handicaps and free drops and general nonsense but Pat McGee's murder was becoming background noise, both Barney and Charlie had been questioned again but nothing new emerged. I heard through Andy Ingles that Randy Hagen had also been questioned but Andy didn't know any details. Considering how Randy had looked at me the last time I spoke to him, I decided against interrogating him again, I would always prefer to keep my head on my shoulders and my face might not be the prettiest but I don't want it rearranged thanks very much.

"Danny, wait up" Sonny Dixon was coming across the golf course car park, gesturing for me to come to him. It was raining, I gave him the finger and shouted "I will see you inside."

"Coffee" I asked him as he came into the kitchen, dripping wet.

"Did you not hear me?" he asked.

"Of course I heard you, did you not see my finger?" I asked.

"I wanted a wee word" he said.

"Microscopic" I replied.

"Naw I mean a quick word" he said.

"Velocity" I replied.

"Gonny fuckin stop it ya fanny" he said.

"Ok" I said.

"My wife's organising a fiftieth birthday party for me" He started to say.

"Bit fucking late, is she no" I said.

"Is it remotely fuckin possible that you can shut the fuck up and listen before anybody else comes in" he asked.

"Probably not, but I'll have a go. Oh and by the way if you are gonny ask me about catering your party because I done Andy's, remember the finger I showed you outside consider it shown again." I said, failing miserably to shut the fuck up as previously agreed.

"Naw, the chef here is catering it, naw, I just wanted to ask your opinion if you thought it was too soon after the McGee incident" he said

"The McGee Incident is it now, is that what we are calling it now, have we stopped referring to it as the Pat McGee skewered on a golf club incident then, that's good, because I thought that was a bit much." I said stoically.

"Your boys right about you, you are a fuckin fanny" he said seriously.

"When did he say that ya lying old bastard, Peter Wouldn't say that" I said, all the time thinking he probably would.

"Oh, did I say your boy, I meant your wife" Sonny said and laughed, Sonny loves his own jokes, probably even more than I love mine.

"If you want my opinion, have your party, what happened, happened. Life goes on, just don't invite Mrs McGee it might bring the mood down" I suggested grinning.

Chapter Eight; Sonny's delight.

I don't suppose it's in the same league as the last night of the proms or New Years Eve in New York, but I got the feeling everybody was quite looking forward to Sonny's shindig at Happy Valley.

"Are you going" Rob chandler asked me as we stood on the first tee on the morning of Sonny's party.

"It's not me to go Rob, It's you" Rob is the old age pensioner Geordie we keep as a pet at Happy Valley. He's an exceptionally nice fella but he doesn't hear everything you say to him, not because he's deaf just because his ears and tongue don't work independently. So when he is talking he can't hear you, which means that for most of the time he can't hear you.

"No no" he laughed and bent over to put his tee in the ground, eventually when he came back up out of breath and red in the face, he continued "I mean to Sonny's party"

"Aw right, Aye, I'll be going, probably as Spiderman, my missus says there's a onesy in Asda for twelve quid. I will get that and go as Spiderman"

"I don't know what you mean" he said to me standing looking at me.

"Take your tee shot, and then we can talk Rob, there's a queue of golfers almost up to the pro shop" I said.

"Why aye man so there is, what are they all waiting for?" he asked.

"You" I replied.

His ball had rolled off the plastic tee so when he eventually stood back up red in the face again after having been down there for a few seconds putting it back on, he appeared ready to take his first shot.

"Spiderman?" he said out loud with a shake of his head and thumped his ball nicely down the middle.

I am pretty sure that I had convinced him by the third hole that Sonny's shindig was fancy dress, if Jasper hadn't spoiled it by later telling him that it wasn't, Rob was going to turn up in an emu costume that he had upstairs in his loft and hadn't worn since 1993.

It was, as usual, a banter filled morning of golf, some aggressive glaring came my way from Walter and Randy Hagen, but nothing I couldn't handle, Peter who was playing with me Rob and Lesley Clifford, did ask what was up with Randy Hagen as he was staring daggers at me all morning, I told him I think Randy might fancy me, all those muscles and tattoos were a dead giveaway to his sexuality, it got a laugh from three of us, Rob was talking about his last shot so didn't hear the joke.

Lesley Clifford played his usual flawless golf and Peter and him beat Rob and me six and five, a bit of a downer on the morning of the big party, but cest la vie, you can't win them all (Although once in a while would be nice).

As I was stowing my clubs away in the upstairs locker room, I was surprised to see Randy Hagen there.

"Alright Shagger, I didn't know you had a locker up here, I thought you were downstairs, have they evicted you?" I asked trying to raise a smile.

He didn't raise a smile "What are you up to Danny" he asked me belligerently.

"I'm struggling to lift my clubs into this high locker and jam my shoes in beside them, what are you up to" I said, sarcastically, turning to face him square on. He swung a punch at me.

Seriously he swung a punch, I was confused and bewildered, and where had this come from? I avoided the punch and leapt over a low bench, putting it between us, I raised my hands in a calm down gesture and said. "What the fucks up with you Shagger, who peed in your Irn bru?"

"You're scheming behind my Da's back trying to get him the blame for McGee, I've heard all your sly remarks and I've heard all about your secret meetings with Stuart Taggart, and it's about time somebody brought you down a peg or two. I know what you are up to, you're trying to blame it on my Da because it was Charlie that done it, and your protecting him because he's in your tin" he said pacing back and forth trying to decide whether to run round the bench or jump over it.

I was momentarily distracted by Jamie McArthur coming into the locker room and then departing in one swift about turn, but it didn't stop me from giggling, which I know was the wrong thing to do when being confronted by a very fit and robust angry young man, if one of his swinging haymakers connected, I could be in a coma for months.

I moved back and forwards along the bench trying to anticipate whether Randy would jump over it or rush round it, I laughed "For fuck sakes Shagger listen to yourself, I'm trying to frame your Da and protect Charlie, because he's in my tin, do you know how stupit that sounds" Wrong word, steam came out of his ears.

I held my hands up again "Whoa, sorry I didnae mean stupit I mean mental, I like your Da, most of the time" I grinned, why can't I stop

134

my mouth saying stupid things even when my life might be in danger. "I'm sorry Shagger but seriously I widnae do that to anybody especially your Da, what's this really about are you frightened your Da might actually have done it?" I asked.

He leapt over the bench almost taking me by surprise, but I managed to twist away from his lunge and leap over the bench in the opposite direction, there was something lying against the wall at the side of my locker and I instinctively grabbed it and brandished it at him.

"Come near me again and I'll use it Shagger, I mean it calm the fuck down before somebody gets hurt" I shouted.

Walter appeared and said "You'll use it for what, a rendition of singing in the rain"

I looked down and seen I was holding a broken golf umbrella, I laughed and said to Walter "Thank fuck you're here, young Shaggers taking a maddy, sort him out will you"

Walter turned to Randy and said "Alright son, do you need a hand"

Randy replied "For this old fat fucker, are you having a laugh Da"

I felt the blood draining from my face and my knees got wobbly "Whoa, hold up Walter, what is the matter with you two, this is going too far" Jamie McArthur had appeared behind Walter and Randy as well as two others, there were surely too many people for this to kick off now. Peter also appeared, his contribution helped a lot.

"If this is going to be a fight I'll have a fiver on Shagger to knock him out with one punch" he said and brushed past me to put his clubs away in his locker. As he did, he took the broken umbrella from my hand and said "Are you going to try and fix this because I think it's buggered"

Peter was stood beside me, there were about half a dozen people standing watching, Shagger wouldn't punch me now, so I could be brave again and shoot my mouth off "No I was just about to ram it up Shaggers arse and open it" I said

I was wrong Shagger could and did punch me, it was only a glancing blow, and it scared me more than it hurt me. Walter and Jamie McArthur dragged him back and prevented him from doing any damage. Peter shook his head and said "Sometimes less is more Da, maybe try shutting up when you're winning eh" he brushed past me again and asked "Did anybody get a two today there's £55 in the kitty"

Everybody drifted out of the locker room bar Walter, "Danny, I know you like a laugh and a bit of banter, but Randy is still really upset about what happened between his ma and me, so maybe keep your jokes for somebody else eh, a guys dead you know, maybe everything isnae as funny as you think it is" he said shaking his head in disappointment.

Walter as always was a gentleman who got to the point with a minimum of fuss, I thought of a witty reply but took Peters advice and shut up, besides Walter is, if anything is even more solidly built than Shagger and a coma would have been the happiest result of him punching me.

Later that afternoon my missus was playing silly buggers about going to Sonny's party.

"I don't even like any of your golf buddies, why would I want to go to their stupid party, they're a bunch of drunks and perverts if you ask me, if they're not staring at a woman's cleavage they're being sick down it, go yourself" she said.

I was determined not to beg, she did this all the time, she secretly wanted to go but I had to be made to beg and persuade her, it wasn't going to happen this time.

"Oh come on, please" I begged.

"Why should I" she said "For that bozo, Jasper Lumphead or whatever he's called to slabber all over me and twist about the dance floor like a demented wino, I don't think so" she said adamantly, whilst at the same time taking all of the makeup she would be needing out of her makeup bag and arranging it in a row in front of her magnifying make up mirror, I was fed up with this begging game.

"Ok, fair enough I will go myself. I'll give Peter a quick phone and let him know you're not going, maybe he needs a babysitter, I'll tell him to bring the three kids along as soon as he likes ok" I said.

She was the length of the kitchen away from me, the phone was three feet in front of me, and she reached it first. "No you bloody well won't, I know your plan. Go without me and dance with all the sexy lady golfers up there, you're not on, I'll come with you but only because I want to keep an eye on you, you canny be trusted when you're drinking"

"I don't drink" I said flummoxed by her logic.

"Aye so you say" she answered flummoxing me again. Her ability to ignore simple facts in the midst of an argument was phenomenal.

We were almost the last couple to turn up, and naturally one of the few places left to sit was at a table with Walter and Randy Hagen. I hesitated, I had no wish to kick things off again and spoil Sonny's party, I looked round the hall. We could possibly squeeze in amongst Sonny's workmates, but they looked even shiftier than the unbearables if that was possible.

Walter stood and put one arm around my shoulder "Come and sit down Danny, Patricia you're looking lovely sweetheart, what would you like to drink?" he said smarmily.

What else could I do but sit down at his table, Randy smiled at me like a bulldog smiles at a cat. I noticed he was on his own again, he claimed to have a girlfriend but nobody I knew had ever seen her, maybe he kept her under his bed beside his bicycle pump.

At least there was the compensation for me of sitting beside luscious Lesley, I mean Walter's fiancé not the club champion, and he isn't luscious, at all. I had heard the rumours about Lesley being a stripper some years ago, again I am talking about Walters fiancé and not the club champion, although I suppose anything is possible. As I looked at her I could see why it was possible she had been a stripper she was fit and very pretty and the secret smiles she launched at me were quite raunchy I suppose if you like that kind of thing.

The party was first class Sonny's missus and family had done him proud, the hall was bedecked in blue red and white balloons with him being a staunch blue nose, I suppose it was to be expected, he sang along with simply the best through the DJ's mike, it lifted the atmosphere quite nicely. The catering was top notch, provided by the golf club kitchen, in short everything was going along very nicely. And then somebody let the dogs out.

"I'm not finished with you" Randy slurred at me across the table. His dad was dancing with my wife and Lesley was dancing with Lesley (work it out for yourself).

I was stone cold sober and desperate to avoid trouble, even though, with Shagger as drunk as he was, it might be the one and only way I could have a fight with him and either win or not get beaten too badly.

"Shagger, son, you've took me the wrong way, I don't think your Da had anything to do with what happened to McGee. Your Da's an absolute gentleman and a scholar, there is no way on earth he would have anything to do with something like that, so do both of us a favour mate, give it a rest, nobody is out to get at your da or fit him up for something he didn't do" I said placating him and reassuring him of my innocence in this situation.

He took a few seconds to take in what I was saying and finally reached a decision. "Ok, ok big man, fair enough, I've been a prat, I know that but I love my Da" (Told you he was drunk)

"I love my Da big man, and he widnae hurt a fly, my Da's a great guy, I love him, and he widnae hurt a fly big man I love him" (very drunk)

"Aye ok shagger I get it, you love him and e widnae hurt a fly, I get it son, I get it" I said taking his hand from my arm where he had an iron grip, apparently he had to hold me in a vice like grip to explain the depth of his love for his Da and that he widnae hurt a fly.

I could see his mind working around a thought, his eyes followed the thought from one side of his brain to the other and he asked me, "If you don't think it was my Da who was it you think did kill McGee then?"

"You" I replied and stood up and walked away as if going to the bar.

He let this settle into his mind for about five seconds and then erupted, flipping the table up and screaming and shouting, thankfully his screams and shouts were indecipherable so nobody knew what his problem was. Some of the drinks he threw in the air when he flipped the table had splashed onto a nearby table which held several of Sonny's workmates, they really were a grim looking bunch, and I wouldn't like to meet any of them in a dark close in Govan on a Friday night.

One or two of them took umbrage at the drink spilling and started remonstrating with Shagger, by this time he was beyond the arguing stage, he was much more in the head butting and kicking and punching stage. All hell broke loose, as they say, if the lounge had batwing doors it couldn't have looked more like a Wild West saloon.

As soon as Shagger threw the first punch and a fat ugly bloke reciprocated catching Randy square on the chin, both Walter and I went for the fat ugly bloke, Walter got there first and decked him with one punch, this then cascaded across the room with the unbearables en masse scrapping with Sonny's workmates, a few of the women were dragged into the fray. Everywhere you looked there were men grappling with each other and women bent double with a grip on each others hair.

I was standing back to back with Walter Hagen in the middle of the worst of the fighting, we were either side of Randy who was struggling to get to his feet, and Walter kept pushing him down and telling him to stay down. We stood there fists raised ready to take on all comers, I turned and nodded at Walter, directing his attention to the buffet table. Jamie McArthur was standing beside

Jasper Lemon and they were both launching sausage rolls and vole au vents at several of Sonny's workmates male and female. They were both laughing to the extent that tears were rolling down their faces, in fact I am sure some of those tears had rolled down as far as Jasper's crotch, well I think it was a tear stain I could see.

The bar staff eventually calmed everybody down, the last to be calmed down was Barry Monk the 75 year old pocket dynamo, he had two young guys in a double head lock banging their heads together, it took four of us to free them, I think that Barry's arms might be made of oak, with a solid steel core, that man is strong.

The whole thing was blamed on Sonny's workmates (mostly by me) and they were ejected. Walter thanked me for stepping in with him and preventing any more damage being done to Randy. I looked at Randy wiping the blood from his nose and mouth and could sense his confusion, he had already forgotten what had actually started him off and he also thanked me, although he did seem very unsure about what he was thanking me for.

The night was over it was time to clear up and count the bruises, Jasper and Jamie were still at the buffet table but this time filling a doggy bag, well who could blame them there was a medal in the morning, and playing a medal raised a hunger in everybody.

I won the second division medal the next day with a seventy six, net sixty four, happy days, it pays to be one of the few sober players on a Sunday morning, more cash for the tin kerching.

Most of the unbearables turned up, Sonny's do was obviously the talk of the steamie that morning, we all had a good laugh about it. Randy hadn't turned up, unsurprisingly, but Walter had and he was at a loss as to knowing what had started the entire furore, in the first place.

"You were sitting with him Danny, what pushed his go crazy button did you notice?" he asked me as we sat having an orange juice in the smokers room after the golf was over.

"I don't know" I said innocently, "I stood up to go to the bar and the next thing I know some big fat ugly guy had stuck one on Randy's chin and the wild west came to Happy Valley, you were dancing with my missus right next to our table, did you not see what got him going loco in Acapulco"

"No I was too busy trying to get your wife's hand off my arse at the time" he said grinning.

"I presume then that you keep your dosh in your back pocket Walter" I said also grinning

Barry Monk was still hyper from the night before "Did you see me get them two thugs son, did you, I had one under each arm banging their heads together, and I was banging my knees up into their face, they'll think twice before messing with us again son, I'll tell you" he said doing all the head banging and knee bashing actions required to tell the story.

"What had they actually done" I asked.

"They were standing at the side of the dance floor son, and one of them said to the other look at that mad old bastard, they were talking about Jack Sharp, Jack was circling in the middle of the floor with his fists up like a prize-fighter, and opposite him was another old boy I don't even know who he was, but he was doing the same as Jack. So I seen that them two young boys were about to attack Jack, so I stepped in and came up behind them and grabbed them both round the neck and started banging their heads together" he again did all the actions with a grimace on his face.

"Just out of curiosity how did you know they were about to attack Jack" Walter asked him.

"I could see it in their eyes son" Barry answered.

"You said you were behind them" I said.

"I got a side view of their faces and I could see it in the set of their shoulders, trust me son I know what I saw, I always know what I see, twenty twenty vision I've got son, trust me" Barry said, pointing two fingers at his eyes and then jabbing them towards me as if he was doing the evil eye thing, made famous by Bobby Ball.

"Who was the old guy Jack was boxing with then" asked Walter.

"It was my Granda" Sonny said "He's ninety two and normally in a wheelchair"

"Go Jack" I said and laughed.

The hilarity became somewhat subdued when Stuart Taggart entered the smokers room, because of the different tensions over the past couple of days I decided to ignore him, both Walter and Charlie and probably big oily glanced at me when entered the room and hopefully noticed me deliberately ignoring him.

I went to the bar, "One more orange juice and then I'm off Charlie, do you want a drink" I asked, he shook his head as did the others I asked. A text came in on my phone, it was from Stuart Taggart, "Meet me in upstairs locker room, NOW" it said, very fucking polite, I thought.

I swallowed the juice almost in a single slurp, "See you all next week guys" I said walking out of the room, I normally tried to raise a smile by saying something witty or clever when I was leaving and Stuart Taggart had killed that idea.

"I hope you know young Shagger is liable to rip my fucking head off if he sees me talking to you" I said with some anger to Stuart as soon as I saw him skulking about the locker room.

"Is he here?" Stuart asked looking very surprised.

"No he isn't but his Da is and that's just as bad" I said glancing at the door as it opened to reveal Jamie McArthur, who looked in shook his head and backed out again. "There we go, the first thing Jamie's gonny do is tell Walter I'm up here talking to you, this is getting beyond a joke, what do you want anyway"

Stuart pursed his lips and said "I need to know if you have heard anything else about Randy Hagen, anything that might cause you to think he was involved in the murder of Pat McGee" he looked as serious as I have ever seen him.

"Why what's happened" I asked.

"I'm the detective, it's me that's asking you questions" he said. Then when I stood silently he sighed and said "We should be lifting him out of his bed at this very moment, we found his DNA on the grip of the golf club that killed Pat McGee"

"You are fuckin joking" I said "I've been winding him up for the last week, saying I thought it was him that killed McGee, for fuck sake, no wonder he's been trying to rip my head off. His old man will be devastated, do you think it really was him?"

"Aye, it disnae look good at all, there's some DNA on the grip of the five iron, strangely the lab rats canny tell if it's from blood or semen it could be either there's so little of it, it's impossible to tell really, my bets on blood or we have got a very sick puppy on our hands, they also found strands of his hair stuck to big oily's bag. And we have got three statements from people who seen him having a drunken argument with McGee, the night he got kebabbed"

"Walters down in the smoking room, are you gonny tell him" I asked.

"No that would get me the jail, and neither can you, I shouldn'y even be talking to you, anyway you haven't answered my question, is there anything else about Randy that you've heard and I should know.

I had to think about it for a few moments, was there anything I could add, was there any other single thing that I could add that would ensure that young Shagger took the blame and went to prison.

"No, nothing at all" I answered.

Stuart just nodded and left, leaving me alone. I sat down on the bench, the bench that Randy Hagen had chased me round the day before. I thought about whether Taggart would ever discover the truth. The truth about how I had scraped Randy's DNA off his bed sheet in the hotel, he's young there's always DNA on the sheets, and planted it on big oily's five iron which I had sneaked into my bag at the eighteenth hole at Loch Green after we had finished playing, the truth about how I had also found strands of Shaggers hair on his brush in his hotel room and how I planted them on big oily's bag. The truth about how I had knocked on Pat McGee's door at four in the morning, and when he opened the door I pushed him straight on to the bed and plunged the shaft of the five iron straight through him. The truth about the head of that five iron being in my loft with my other trophies.

Will they ever discover the reasons that McGee had to die, the two reasons that he had to die? When Peter, my oldest son, said he wanted to run the unbearables, I decided that he was going to, when my children ask for something I do my best to provide it, I'm a good father. But the main reason he had to die was that he disrespected my beliefs, he should never have said he was going to vote no in the referendum.

THE END

Afterword;

I do hope I haven't offended any of my friends in the real unbearables or any innocent bystanders, beyond the point I can't buy them a drink and laugh it off, if I have, I apologise in advance, it's just for a giggle let it go.

THE UNBEARABLES AND THEIR NICKNAMES

NAME	NICKNAME
Danny mcallister	The councillor
Peter mcallister	Nikey
Charlie gilhooley	Cavalier (laughing)
Barney piper	Big oily (initials BP)
Billy Paterson	Wee oily (initial bp)
Jack sharp	Gentleman jack
David simpson	The part timer
Andy ingles	The fat controller
Jamie mcarthur	The conductor
Jasper lemon	bozo
Igor Currie	Chubby
Barry monk	Hawkeye
Rob Chandler	The Geordie
Jason mckechnie	The quiet man
Lesley Clifford	The claw (his grip)
Farqhuarson Dixon	Tea bag
Walter hagen	The jannie
Randy hagen	shagger
Harry caravan	The snail
Bart cooper	The fat ugly bin man
Stuart Taggart	Porky one
Baxter Carter	Porky two
Ivan Bentley	Smiler
Ingram Houston	Squidward/the spanner.
Pat McGee	Our great leader
Simon Temple	Popeye (the sailorman)
Gary Royal	Bra strap

Printed in Great Britain
by Amazon.co.uk, Ltd.,
Marston Gate.